Sea Sickness

We watched the police divers unload the dinghy. One of the divers removed his hood to shed his face mask for a deep breath of fresh air and promptly threw up into the sea. The noxious stench emanating from the body sent everyone on the narrow boardwalk running back to Dockside. Before a blanket was put into service as a shroud, I glanced at the body and gasped when I saw the battered, bloated face of the homeless woman known as the spitter.

Then, like the diver, I tossed my cookies into the sea.

MORE MYSTERIES FROM THE
BERKLEY PUBLISHING GROUP . . .

Death Rides
an
Ill Wind

Kate Grilley

BERKLEY PRIME CRIME, NEW YORK

DEATH RIDES AN ILL WIND

A Berkley Prime Crime Book / published by arrangement with the author

PRINTING HISTORY
Berkley Prime Crime edition / April 2001

ISBN: 0-425-17930-3

Berkley Prime Crime Books are published
by The Berkley Publishing Group,
a division of Penguin Putnam Inc.,
375 Hudson Street, New York, New York 10014.
The name BERKLEY PRIME CRIME and the BERKLEY PRIME CRIME
design are trademarks belonging to Penguin Putnam Inc.

PRINTED IN THE UNITED STATES OF AMERICA

10 9 8 7 6 5 4 3 2 1

For Sue Henry,
Joyce Christmas and Dorian Yeager . . .
together wherever we go.

Death Rides
an
Ill Wind

Chapter
1

"IT'S TOO DAMNED hot."

Abby drained the last of her iced coffee, signaled the Watering Hole waitress for a refill, then leaned back in her chair, fanning her face with her hand.

"Abby, you're not going to sing about the heat, are you?" said Margo, pausing to glare in my direction. "Kel, you've got to stop playing that Mel Tormé number from *Kiss Me, Kate* on your radio show every single morning. It's making me stark raving CRAZY." She shouted the final word, then lowered her voice and continued, sounding like she was talking through clenched teeth. "We all KNOW it's hot. It's BEEN hot since early May."

"I hear you," I said, the voice of sweetness and reason. "You're right. We've had enough Cole Porter. Tomorrow I'll open with Irving Berlin. You'll love Ella Fitzgerald's 'Heat Wave.' " I ducked when Margo threw her balled-up napkin at me.

Margo, Abby and I were finishing a Monday lunch at our permanently reserved table outside the Watering Hole, directly across from Margo's Island Palms Real Estate office and Abby's adjacent law office above the toy store. The round wooden table with its aging captain's chairs was our weekday clubhouse where Abby, Margo, Jerry and Pete had morning coffee while I was on the air at WBZE doing my radio show from 6 A.M. 'til noon. It was also the place we usually met for lunch and occasionally for late-afternoon drinks. Jerry once calculated we'd spent enough money at the Watering Hole to buy it five times over; but if we owned it, we'd probably go broke by being our own best customers.

"What's the latest weather forecast?" asked Abby.

"NOAA in San Juan says SOS and that doesn't mean save our ships," I replied with a grin. "Highs in the upper nineties, chance of rain less than twenty percent, more sand blowing off the Sahara into the upper atmosphere. Same old, same old. Don't ask about the heat index. It's right up there with a body fever that will fry your brain." I picked up Margo's napkin to dab at the sweat dripping off my gamin-cut hair into my ears.

From under the fading yellow canvas umbrella, we looked down the palm-tree-lined cobblestone walkway toward the seaside boardwalk that skirted downtown Isabeya. Sand-laden haze, suspended in the air like a gauze scrim between sky and ocean, obscured any view of the out-islands forty miles north of St. Chris. Telltales drooped like overcooked linguini on the smattering of sailboats moored in the Isabeya harbor in a placid Caribbean Sea that shimmered like peacock-hued Carnival glass.

"August. I hate August," said Margo. "It's the middle of hurricane season, there are no tourists and my real estate sales are down the tubes. I'm so bored I could sort Paul's socks for mental stimulation. Thank God Labor Day is only a week away. Maybe it'll finally start cooling off." She tucked a loose strand of blond hair back into her heat-beating French braid. "What are you two doing this afternoon?"

"I'm drafting a motion for court tomorrow," said Abby.

"I'm going home to wallow under my ceiling fan with Minx and chill out watching *Dr. Zhivago* on video," I said. "If you want to join me, I'll treat you to a frosty gin and tonic. It'll be more fun than sorting socks."

"Kel, you can't fool me," said Margo. "You're going home to drool over Omar Sharif. I know you didn't go to Egypt last year just to see the Sphinx and pyramids. No one goes to Egypt in August except a penny-pincher like you. Too bad Omar was playing bridge in Paris at the time."

A retort died on my tongue when a grubby hand snaked around my shoulder to snatch my dripping glass of watered-down tea from the table.

"What the hell?" I whipped around to see an unkempt woman, possibly in her late twenties, pour the contents of my glass into a tattered paper cup. She tossed the glass into a nearby shrub, spit in my general direction, then hotfooted over the cobblestones toward the boardwalk. The entire incident, from snatch to sprint, took less than ten seconds.

Carole, the Watering Hole waitress, ran to our table. "Kelly, I'll bring you a fresh iced tea. On the house." She retrieved the empty glass from the bush and returned with a round for the table.

"Who or what was that?" I asked, stirring Sweet'n Low into my tea.

"I call her the spitter," said Carole. "She's been hanging around for a couple of weeks. I figure she's either a druggie or a flipped-out mental case. She seldom says anything, just spits and runs. We try to keep her away from the customers, but she works fast."

"Have you told the cops about her?" I asked.

"Yeah, but it doesn't do any good. She's invisible when

they're around. One night after closing I saw her rum-
maging through the Dumpster outside the kitchen."

I pulled a ten-dollar bill from my wallet and handed it
to Carole with my lunch tab and tip. "Her next meal's on
me."

"Kel, are you nuts?" said Margo. "Why encourage
someone like that? She belongs in rehab. Let them take
care of her."

"There but for the grace of God . . ." I was interrupted
before I could finish my thought.

"I do declare. Some things never change. Here y'all are
having lunch at the round table just like old times."

Margo and I stared through our sunglasses at the ap-
parition of a redheaded woman in her mid-thirties clad in
a girlish white-eyelet sundress approaching our table on
improbable spike-heeled sling-back sandals. The sweat
trickling off my ears suddenly felt frozen to my earlobes.

Abby was the first to find her voice. "Leila Mae Turner.
What brings you back to St. Chris?"

Without waiting for an invitation, Leila Mae seated herself next to Abby, placing her left hand on Abby's fore-
arm. "It's so good to see y'all again."

We were all made very aware of the emerald-cut rock
glittering on Leila Mae's fourth finger, eclipsing Abby's
trademark two-carat flawless diamond studs. Abby dis-
creetly shook off Leila Mae's hand by reaching for her
fresh glass of iced coffee.

"It's Baroness Thorsen now," Leila Mae twittered.
"The baron and I arrived this morning for a belated hon-
eymoon. Christian has family business on St. Chris that
needs looking after. His great-great-great . . ." She
stopped talking to count on her fingers, then threw her
hands in the air. "Well, I never could keep track of all
those greats, but a distant grandfather . . . on his father's
side? From Denmark? Christian said his great-granddaddy
was a sea captain and actually died here. Can you imag-

ine? It was about the time of that horrid War of Northern Aggression that caused such hardship for my family back in Savannah. When Christian and I discovered we both had ties to St. Chris? I declare, it was a match made in heaven."

Abby responded politely. "Where are you staying? Dockside?"

Leila Mae smiled, a smug little smile. "Mercy no, Abby. We're at Harborview. But Daddy's sending his yacht down from Savannah. Isn't he the sweetest? Y'all must come out for drinks one night real soon." She rose from the table as sinuously as a cobra emerging from its basket. "I'd love to stay and chat, but Christian really hates to be kept waiting." She circled the table to lay a hand first on Margo's shoulder—"How's Paul, Margo? You're looking as divine as ever"—then on mine. "Kelly, I swear you haven't changed one teensy bit in five years. Do give my love to Peter." Leila Mae waggled her acrylic-nailed fingertips, lacquered in a shade one could only describe as Pepto-Bismol pink. "Bye-bye now."

We silently tracked Leila Mae's departure, exhaling *en masse* when she was finally out of sight. Margo began singing "Hard Hearted Hannah (the vamp of Savannah)" under her breath.

"Honey chile," said Abby, layering a thick drawl atop her crisp New England accent, "I do believe Emmy Slattery has come back to Tara."

"Kel, forget chilling out with Omar," said Margo, reaching for her purse. "I hope you've got plenty of ice stashed in your freezer. Grab your laptop, Abby. You can draft your motion at Kelly's house. I predict it's going to get very drunk out this afternoon."

Chapter
2

SEPTEMBER 10 IS the height of the tropical Atlantic hurricane season. Eleven days before the annual peak a small cluster of clouds slid off the West African coast into a low-pressure trough southeast of the Cape Verde Islands. The amorphous clouds drifted lazily aloft, suckling from the unseasonably warm ocean waters below, growing fatter with each moisture-laden updraft. The National Hurricane Center in Miami was too busy tracking a budding storm in the Gulf of Mexico to pay any attention to what would become Tropical Depression Number Seven.

Driving to the WBZE studio at five-thirty in the morning with a crashing hangover was not a great way to jump-start a workday.

Sweet baby Minx, my calico cat, had done her best to wake me gently before the alarm went off at four-thirty, but the tapping of her paw on my cheek set off a volley of cannon balls exploding in my head. I lurched to the loo, ransacked my medicine cabinet for a handful of generic painkillers and washed them down with an Alka-Seltzer chaser before stumbling into the kitchen to feed Minx.

The sight of an empty gin bottle listing in my kitchen sink along with three thermal glasses, dried out key lime wedges and enough dead tonic bottles to ward off malaria in a small third-world nation reminded me that paybacks are hell, as Margo would soon discover. Living in the land of duty-free liquor meant I'd spent more on tonic than the bottle of Tanqueray. At least the limes were free, picked from the trees growing on my property.

"Yo, Mama." Michael, the 10 P.M. to 6 A.M. deejay, greeted me with an ear-shattering bellow followed by a spine-adjusting hug and a vampire kiss planted on my neck. "Did your cistern run dry? You reek of bathtub gin."

"Blame Margo. It was all her fault. She kept insisting on one for the road," I said, heading for the music library to pull the music for my six-hour show. "Where did we put Verdi's *Requiem*?"

Michael followed on my heels. "Who died?"

"My brain. Who's been messing in the music library? I can't find anything this morning." I grabbed an album off the shelf. "I'll make do with Ravel. Margo speaks French, she'll get the message."

I stopped to grab the news copy off the Teletype machine and pull a Tab from the six-pack nestled in my portable cooler. It was going to be a very long and very thirsty morning.

After the six o'clock news I opened my show with Ella Fitzgerald, followed by a brief intro for Maurice Ravel's *Pavane pour une enfante défunte*. The phone rang the second the music started.

"Good morning, WBZE, the breath of fresh music in the Caribbean."

"Kel, you really are too twisted for words," said Margo. "Dead princess, my ass. You'd better not be blaming me for yesterday afternoon. Does your head hurt as much as mine?"

"I feel great," I said, cradling the phone between my neck and shoulder while I dug for the battered roll of Tums lurking in the depths of my tote.

"Liar. I hope your nose grows. Don't call me at the office this morning. I'm taking a mental-health day and going back to bed. Come over to Sea Breezes when you're through with work and I'll treat you to a Bloody and lunch at Port in a Storm."

Michael sauntered back into the studio with an album in his hand. "Here. Someone filed it under G instead of V."

I flashed him a grateful smile. We both knew that someone was Emily, our receptionist. Emily isn't the brightest bulb in the chandelier, but she is the granddaughter of Mrs. H, WBZE'S globe-trotting owner. "Thanks. You didn't have to stay late to find this for me. You must be starving." When McDonald's opened its doors at six, Michael was usually the first at the counter, ordering his bedtime snack.

"What were you and Rapunzel up to last night?"

"A girl thing." I knew how stupid and evasive I sounded.

"Don't pull that 'I've got a secret' crap, Mama. It pisses me off. You know we have no secrets. If it's none of my business, that's cool, but don't be cute about it. I hate cute. Especially from a broad who's so hungover she's still wearing her sunglasses." Michael flipped the switch to douse the overhead fluorescents, leaving the studio lit only by the console dials and the early-morning light filtering through the security grille covering the plate-glass picture window. "Better?"

"Much. Thanks." I knew my eyes looked like something from a mutant alien horror movie, so I kept my sunglasses firmly in place. "Margo and I killed a fresh fifth of Tanqueray. Abby helped, but she went home before we finished the job."

"What were you celebrating? Did Margo finally peddle some real estate?"

"In her dreams. We had a surprise at lunch yesterday. Someone we all knew years ago is back on-island."

"Anyone I know?" said Michael.

"You've been on St. Chris *how* long? Two and a half years? Before your time."

"When do I get to meet him?"

"It's not a him, Michael. I hope you two never meet."

"Why not? In the six months we've been a duo I've met all your friends."

"Trust me, Michael, this is no friend. This is the bitch who destroyed my fifteen-year marriage to Pete. Can we drop it? My head hurts, and I've got a show to do."

Michael made a big production of tiptoeing out of the studio. But not before he wrapped his arms around me in a gentle hug, whispered in my ear, then planted a soft kiss on the back of my neck.

"You told Michael about Leila Mae? In those words?" Margo eyed me over the top of her sunglasses before taking a generous swig of her Bloody Mary. We were on our first. For medicinal purposes. Mitch, the bartender, had strict orders to cut us off after the second round.

We were seated at a table for two inside Port in a Storm, the seaside bar and restaurant at Sea Breezes where Margo and Paul shared a condo on the middle floor of the three-story complex. The restaurant ceiling fans twirled on medium, generating enough breeze to keep the sultry air moving without blowing food off the tables.

"Exactly those words," I said, draining the liquid in the squat tumbler to the halfway mark. "Where was this when I needed it at five this morning?" At the bar Mitch began filling two clean glasses with crushed ice.

"What did Michael say?"

I stifled a giggle. "He said, and I quote, 'the bitch deserves a medal for getting that prick out of your life.' Have you told Paul yet?"

"I haven't talked to him since yesterday morning. He spent last night in Antigua on a charter. He'll be back late this afternoon; I'll tell him then. Don't forget we're all going to the blue moon barbeque at the Lower Deck tonight."

"Michael said he'd meet me there at six-thirty." I fished a square buff envelope from my purse and waved it at Margo. "What are you going to do about this invitation for drinks Saturday night? You *did* receive one?"

"Jerry said there was one waiting for me at the office. One for him, one for Pete and one for me. Abby called after court to say she got one, too."

I refrained from comment until Mitch put our fresh drinks on the table and carried the used glasses back to the bar. "What is Leila Mae up to now? Doesn't she realize that everyone she invited to that party hates her guts?"

Margo smiled as she picked up her drink.

"I'll tell you right now," I said, "I'm not going to that damned party. What you do is your business, but I'm staying home."

"Oh no you're not" said Margo. "You and I are in this together. I don't care if Paul's affair with Leila Mae was over long before he and I got together: I don't want him within a mile of that man-eating spider. Tell you what. You and Michael are coming to our house for dinner Saturday night. We're grilling steaks on the gallery. We arranged it last week, remember?"

"You're on, kid," I replied, as I opened the lunch menu. "Wild horses couldn't keep me away."

Chapter

3

THE NATIONAL WEATHER Service was focused on the Gulf of Mexico, where Fred—having barely achieved named-tropical-storm status, with maximum sustained winds of forty-one miles per hour—was heading for landfall on the Texas-Louisiana coastline. It appeared to viewers of the Weather Channel's *Tropical Update* that the world dropped off into uncharted oblivion east of Florida, where medieval European cartographers had once lettered "here there be dragons." But southeast of the Cape Verde Islands, an infant dragon was drawing breath to spit thunder and lightning as it took a tentative step westward.

The Lower Deck restaurant at Dockside—a hotel and restaurant complex built in a native stone warehouse dating back to the days when pirates roamed the Caribbean Sea—was jumping. When Michael and I both arrived at six-thirty, the air was filled with meat-scented smoke from sizzling ribs on large open grills, and the sound of a scratchy band playing—what else?—"Blue Moon." We made our way through throngs of chatting diners to the table where Margo and Paul were hoisting frosty mugs of beer.

"You made it just in time," said Margo. "Victoria says draft beer is half price until the moon rises. Hurry up and get your order in."

"Where's Vic?" I asked.

"Upstairs in her office with Abby. Looked like serious business to me."

We were watching the cloudless eastern sky fade to black when Jerry sauntered toward us from the waterfront boardwalk. He snagged a chair from a nearby table and wedged his way between Margo and Michael.

"Hey, Jerry," said Margo, "what brings you out? I thought you weren't allowed on the streets until after dark."

"I vant to suck your blood," said Jerry, baring his fangs at Margo in a bad Bela Lugosi imitation. "But I'll settle for a drink."

"Put the bite on Kelly," replied Margo. "You still owe me three drinks from last week."

I smiled to myself and told the waitress I'd buy Jerry a drink. Jerry was notorious for the moths in his wallet and cavalier "I'll catch you another time" payback promises.

After ordering his usual rum and water—"I'll have a white on white on the rocks; better make that a double"— Jerry began nibbling the plantain chips and mango salsa we'd ordered for an appetizer—this after telling Margo he and Heidi had already eaten dinner.

"Are we all ready for the big shindig Saturday night?" Jerry asked.

"Count me out," I said. "I've got plans to watch paint dry." Michael shot me a questioning look, which I ignored.

"I'm rotating my tires," said Margo, moving the appetizer basket out of Jerry's reach.

"Hi, guys, is there room for one more?"

"Have a seat, Abby," said Jerry, "but you gotta find your own chair."

Paul and I moved to make room for Abby while Michael went off in search of an unoccupied chair.

"I'm starving," said Abby, reaching for the appetizer basket. "It's been a long day and I'm too tired to go home and cook. I could smell the barbeque from Victoria's office."

"Where is Vic?" I asked. "She's usually down here for barbeque night."

"She's doing some paperwork in her office," replied Abby. "She may be down later."

The full moon, looking like a blood orange, rose slowly, teasingly, over the east-end hills. A clanging bell informed us the draft beer special had ended. We gazed at the moon in momentary silence, then went to the buffet, leaving Jerry to guard our table.

When we returned with plates full of ribs, corn, salad and garlic bread, we'd been joined by Pete, my former husband, and Angie, his young bride of almost six months.

"My God, Angie," said Margo, "you look like you're about to burst. When is the baby due?"

"Not for another month," replied Angie with a sigh, "but I'm ready now. It doesn't matter if I sit, stand or lie down. I can't get comfortable. Why didn't someone tell me?"

"Don't look at us," said Abby. "You're the only mother-to-be at this table. The rest of us never had kids."

"Enough baby talk," said Jerry, picking up a fresh drink. "Let's get back to Saturday night. Who's going to the party?"

"What party?" asked Angie, turning to Pete. His mouth was too full of barbeque to respond.

"Looks like you're going to be a crowd of one, Jerry,"

said Margo with a grin. "But we all know you'd go to the opening of an envelope. Especially if there's free food and booze involved."

Ignoring Margo's pointed retort, Jerry looked over our heads at a couple boarding the Harborview-bound ferry idling at the dock. "There's the happy couple now. I never knew Leila went for older men." Jerry sat up straight and smoothed what was left of his hair. If he'd been a peacock, he would have puffed his chest and spread his tail.

"Where?" said Margo, turning to peer at the boardwalk. "I've never seen a count up close before."

"He's not a count," I muttered. "Christian is only a baron."

Jerry put two fingers in his mouth and let loose with an ear-shattering whistle.

Leila Mae looked startled, but waved as the captain cast off the ropes in preparation for crossing the three hundred feet of ocean to Harborview. She turned her head away from us to say something over her shoulder, then jumped off the ferry onto the dock and headed in our direction.

"Will someone please tell me what's going on?" said Angie. "If I don't get some answers, I'm going to start kicking ass and taking names."

I got up to head for the loo before Leila Mae reached the table.

"Wait up, Kel." Angie made her way through the crowd as fast as she could waddle. "I spend half my life in the john these days."

After we'd waited our turn in the queue, Angie said, "Is there someplace we can talk?"

"Can you manage a flight of stairs?"

"If I take it slow and easy."

We went upstairs to the Posh Nosh bar, away from the noise of the courtyard below. The bar was empty, shut down for the evening because of the barbeque. The door to Victoria's office was closed with a Do Not Disturb sign hanging from the knob.

"Kel, I know this is a sore subject, but I really want to apologize for last spring. It wasn't your fault I got suspended from the police force. When I found out I was pregnant my whole life turned upside down. I made Pete crazy, and he said some stupid things. Please forgive me."

"Angie, it's forgiven and forgotten." I looked down into the courtyard where Leila Mae was standing next to Pete's chair with her hand resting on his shoulder.

"Who is that woman?"

"The original Venus flytrap."

"I'd better go down and defend my turf," said Angie. "Will you help me get up?"

As Angie grabbed my hand to pull herself out of the chair, a grimace clouded her face.

"I don't think I can get up right now," she said. "I don't feel very well."

"What's the matter?" I said. "Something you ate?"

"I hope so," she replied, sweat beading her forehead. "Please, get Pete up here."

I ran down the stairs to our table, edging Leila Mae aside to whisper in Pete's ear. We sprinted up to the bar where Angie was still seated, breathing rapidly through her mouth while sweat poured down her face.

"Kelly, if you upset my wife, I swear . . ."

"Honey, shut up and get me to the hospital. I think I'm in labor." Angie gripped the chair arms. "Now. I need to go now."

Pete stood frozen to his spot, like in a game of statue maker, staring at his bride.

"Angie, hang on," I said. "I'll be right back. I'm going for reinforcements."

I flew back to the table. Abby, Margo, Paul, Jerry and Michael raced behind me up to the Posh Nosh bar, deserting Leila Mae without a backward glance.

Chapter
4

"ARE YOU AN aunt yet?" were the first words out of Michael's mouth when I walked bleary-eyed into the station at five-forty Wednesday morning.

"False alarm. Angie was sent home from the hospital early this morning. For the record, Pete and I are no longer related, and even if we were, I wouldn't be an aunt."

"Just checking to see if you were firing on all cylinders, Mama. Here's something that'll open your eyes. It came over the wire a few minutes ago." Michael handed me the 5 A.M. weather bulletin from San Juan.

I popped open a Tab, then quickly scanned the page. The tropical weather summary ended with details on Tropical Depression Number Seven and the words "further strengthening expected."

"Michael, that's typical CYA weather talk. We go through this at least once every summer, but it never amounts to anything. Where's the hurricane map?"

"In the music library."

"Bring it in here. We'll plot the track, and you'll see there's nothing to get excited about."

Michael carried the metal tracking map into the studio and hung it on the wall. I dug out the box of pencil-eraser-sized magnets. Michael read off coordinates while I placed magnets on the map, then stood back to admire my handiwork.

The three points formed a line aimed at Tobago, northeast of Venezuela and far, far south of St. Chris.

"See?" I scanned the weather bulletin a second time and refrained from saying "I told you so" but added "why didn't I know about this yesterday morning?"

"Mama, you didn't know your own name yesterday morning. Get a grip; the storm didn't crank up until last night."

I went to the computer in the reception area, opened the hurricane program and plotted the course on-screen. The twelve-hour projection stayed right on the Tobago target. I printed the page and went back into the studio.

"What's the word, Mama? Is it time to alert the troops?"

"Not yet. It's only a tropical depression, and there's still a lot of ocean to cover before it's breathing down our necks. Chill out. It'll probably fizzle long before it gets close to us."

"Works for me. Rain, rain, go away." Michael kissed me a tender good night. "I'm whipped, Mama. I'm going to grab some java and head home. Call you later." I heard the front door slam shut before he roared away on his Harley.

After Ella crooned "Heat Wave," which I played only because I knew it would annoy Margo, I opened the morning classics with Seiji Ozawa conducting the Boston Symphony Orchestra in a recording of Carl Orff's *Carmina Burana*. The 63:11 playing time gave me plenty of un-

interrupted time to get my ducks in order. As the lusty
opening chorus of "O fortuna" filled the studio, I sat down
with the station Rolodex and a clipboard with a fresh legal
pad and began making lists: one for work, one for home.

On the station list:

—call San Juan and Miami for weather updates,
—order extra fuel for generator

There was no need to set up a work schedule. If TD
#7 came close to St. Chris, the staff would be on storm
leave while Minx and I holed up at the station for the
duration. That's the downside to being the general manager of a radio station. To paraphrase Harry Truman:
When the heat's on, everyone else gets out of the kitchen.
Truman also said "the buck stops here," but as Mrs. H
was still on her six-month 'round the world cruise, any
talk of money would have to wait until she was back on
St. Chris at the end of September.

My home list was considerably longer:

—put up hurricane shutters
—disconnect downspouts
—stock up on Tab, toilet paper, cat food and canned
  goods
—set up litter box for Minx
—get gas for car, check tires
—clean off gallery
—get cash for emergencies
—move Top Banana off the beach
—find flashlights, shortwave radio
—buy batteries!!!! (AAA, AA, C and D)
—buy cell phone?

When *Carmina Burana* was in its "O fortuna" reprise finale, I thought about how to present the weather information in the upcoming newscast. Forget the Chicken Little approach—the storm was still twenty-three hundred miles away and our cloudless blue sky was far from falling. There was only one way to handle it. Straightforward and factual. I ended the news by saying:

"The National Weather Service is tracking the progress of a tropical disturbance off the coast of Africa, near the Cape Verde Islands. Further strengthening is expected in the next twenty-four hours. Stay tuned to WBZE for weather updates as they occur. Free weather-tracking maps are available from our advertisers or the WBZE office. We'll be back with more music after this word from Soup to Nuts."

I speed-dialed the National Hurricane Center in Miami to arrange for live on-air updates if the storm course shifted our way, while adding bottled water to both of my lists.

Emily arrived for work at eight-thirty to find a printed list on her desk, complete with local phone numbers for ordering bottled water and generator fuel.

I put out a box of hurricane-tracking maps in the reception area. When I left the station at twelve-fifteen the box was full. According to the 11 A.M. update, the storm was still only a tropical depression with maximum sustained winds of 35 mph. I took another box of maps to drop off in town and headed to the Watering Hole for lunch.

Jerry and Margo were gearing up to leave Island Palms Real Estate for the fifteen-foot trek to the round table when I dropped off hurricane maps at their office.

"What's going on? Is there a storm out there?" asked Jerry.

"So far it's only a depression," I replied, "but I said on my show this morning that free tracking maps were available from our advertisers, and I didn't want you to feel left out. I hate it when you pout."

"I'll take one home to Heidi," said Jerry. "Let me know if this turns into something I should worry about. Margo, remind me to call my insurance agent."

"Write your own reminder, Jerry," said Margo. "What do I look like? A Kelly girl?"

"Excuse me?" I said.

"Sorry, Kel, figure of speech."

We took our usual seats at the round table, scanned the chalkboard for the daily specials and placed our orders.

"Where's your list, Kel?" said Margo.

"List? What list? What are you talking about?"

"You always have a list. You're the most compulsive person I know."

"Better safe than sorry."

"Spare me the clichés," said Jerry. "You two are worse than a daytime talk show."

"Where's Pete?" I asked.

"Home with Angie," said Margo.

"If he's going to stay home until the baby's born, I get first crack at his floor time," said Jerry. "I haven't had a decent sale in weeks."

"But you've cut three strokes off your golf game," said Margo.

"I do a lot of business on the course," said Jerry.

"Especially at the nineteenth hole," I remarked.

The conversation lulled when Carole brought our lunches. "Kel, see me before you leave, okay? Did you bring us those maps?"

"I put a stack of maps on the bar. Let me know if you need more."

Jerry departed when he'd finished his cheeseburger. "I've got a two o'clock tee time. Tell Carole to put my lunch on my tab."

"Kel, do you really think there's a storm coming?" asked Margo.

"Hard to tell; it's pretty far south right now. The computer projection says it's at least three days away."

"What are you doing this afternoon?"

"I need to stop at the market."

"I knew it. You *do* have a list. You usually shop every other Saturday morning."

"It's like Christmas. Shop early, beat the rush. You know how it is here."

"Tell me about it. I haven't been able to find unsalted Lurpak Danish butter in weeks. If you see any, buy five pounds for me. Butter freezes well, and I want to make béarnaise sauce for our steaks Saturday night. I'd go with you, but I'm the only one in the office this afternoon."

"It's lonely at the top," I said.

"Especially with a secretary on vacation, a partner with a pregnant wife and another partner who would rather putt than work. I've gotta go. There's a couple coming in to check condo listings. Call me later." Margo put some money on the table to cover her lunch, and I went to settle up with Carole.

"Kel, the spitter was around late yesterday afternoon. I gave her a meal, like you said, and she left something behind. I think she meant this for you." In Carole's outstretched hand was a wadded grimy tissue, wrapped with a piece of tape. "I wasn't about to open it. Who knows where that's been."

"Thanks." I gingerly picked it up with my fingertips and dropped it in my purse, then headed to my car for more hurricane maps.

After checking my mailbox at the post office and finding only spiderwebs, which meant the first of the month bills hadn't yet been sorted, I stopped at Dockside to leave some maps for Victoria.

She was sitting in her office next to the hotel reception desk. A ceiling fan whirred on low, and the closed shutters made the room feel deliciously cool. Outside the sun was hot enough to blister bare skin.

"Hi, Vic. Smashing barbeque last night. I missed seeing you." Victoria looked like she hadn't slept in a week. "Are you okay?"

"Kelly. How nice. Please sit down. Would you like something cool to drink?" Victoria poured each of us a glass of ice water from the carafe on her desk. "I can offer you something stronger if you'd prefer it."

"No thanks, this is perfect."

"I understand we had some excitement last evening. How is Angelita? Did she have the baby?"

"Not yet; it was a false alarm. Or a good diversionary tactic."

Victoria smiled wanly. "I heard we have a visitor. Fortunately, I have not yet laid eyes on her myself. I've been rather preoccupied with other matters." Victoria's hand trembled as she carefully set her glass on the desk.

"Vic, if you want to talk, you know you can trust me."

Victoria's clear gray eyes met mine. "I could use a friendly ear right now. Other than a solicitor or an accountant."

"You were here for me that night five years ago when I found Pete in our bed with Leila Mae. Talk to me, Vic."

Victoria took a deep breath. "My note has been called." She looked like she needed something stronger than ice water to calm her nerves.

"I'll take you up on that drink offer," I said. Victoria excused herself to go to the Posh Nosh bar, returning with two crystal glasses filled with Tanqueray and tonic, garnished with slices of freshly cut lime.

"Cheers."

"Cheers. Now tell me what happened."

"When I bought the hotel, I put every pound I had into

the down payment, and the previous owner took back a short-term mortgage for the balance. Interest only for ten years based on a twenty-five-year payout with a balloon payment due at the end of the term. I signed the note knowing I had ten years to make a go of this place and could build up my cash reserves while I sought long-term financing."

"But you bought the hotel seven years ago. Haven't you got three years to go on the payout?"

"Under normal circumstances, yes. But it was a demand note. Interest rates are much higher today than they were seven years ago. I have thirty days to pay off the note or I'll lose my hotel."

"Vic, exactly how much money are we talking about?"

"I need four hundred thousand dollars by October 1."

Chapter
5

TD #7 ACHIEVED tropical storm status at 11 P.M. Wednesday and was officially named Gilda. She was still on a due west path heading toward Tobago and further strengthening was anticipated. At 5 A.M. Thursday maximum sustained winds had increased to forty-six miles per hour as Gilda maintained her westerly course.

Emily had followed my instructions to the letter and bills for bottled water and generator fuel were attached to checks waiting for my signature. I signed the checks, feeling a little bit like the boy who cried wolf.

I felt even more foolish when I realized I'd spent almost eight hundred dollars out of my own checkbook Wednesday afternoon—an even thousand if I counted the extra cash I'd withdrawn from the bank for emergencies and stashed in my home floor safe—on groceries, a small gas-powered generator, a cellular phone and enough batteries to ensure Duracell a profitable third quarter. Margo would have a good laugh over my folly. But what she didn't know couldn't hurt me. I certainly wasn't going to mention the twenty-five-pound bag of kitty litter that was still sitting in my car.

Michael bounded out of the studio to greet me with a warm hug and a good-morning kiss.

"Mama, do you know what today is?"

I raised my left wrist close to my nose to peer at the pinhead-sized date window on my watch.

"It's the second." A fast glance at a wall calendar confirmed the month. "Of September. Why?"

"I just wondered if you knew. The Labor Day weekend is upon us. Mama, whaddya say we party? You were dead on about the storm. It's not coming anywhere close. Let's get off the rock for the weekend. Hop over to St. Martin and go skinny-dipping at the nude beach on the French side."

"We're having dinner with Margo and Paul at Sea Breezes Saturday night."

"I thought we were invited to a party that night at Harborview? The one Jerry was talking about at the barbeque."

"Ix-nay on that, Michael."

"Your call, Mama. Can't you get us out of dinner? Or switch it to Friday night? I want to go away this weekend. Just the two of us. How about it?" Michael put his arms around my waist and pulled me close for a kiss.

When my breathing slowed to normal, I murmured, "You are a silver-tongued devil." Michael said nothing, just stood with his arms around my waist grinning at me. "Okay, okay. I'll call Margo this morning. The dinner was to give us all an excuse to avoid Leila Mae's party."

"We'll leave Saturday morning the very second I get off the air. Pack your bag, pick me up at six. I'll leave my bike here at the station, and we'll take your car to the airport."

"That's a plan."

"I'm ready to kick-start the weekend. Meet me tonight

at the ferry at six-thirty. Wear your glad rags, Mama."

"What's the occasion?"

"That's for me to know and you to find out." Michael pushed his Harley out the door while merrily whistling "Moon River."

Breakfast at Tiffany's? I would have thought the *From Here to Eternity* theme was more appropriate to our weekend plans. But I realized there was no accounting for Michael's musical tastes as I hauled a pile of hard rock and heavy metal albums back to the music room for refiling and pulled a recording of Mendelssohn's *Music to A Midsummer Night's Dream* to air on the morning classics.

Michael's taunt, 'That's for me to know and you to find out,' was bugging the hell out of me. Had I forgotten something really important? I pulled my date book from my tote and the grimy wad of tape-sealed tissue fell to the floor with a faint clink. After checking my calendar—Michael's birthday wasn't until the end of October, so I hadn't forgotten that—I turned my attention to the object on the floor.

You don't know where that tissue's been, I thought as I reached for a letter opener to lift the object onto the console.

Wielding a letter opener and scissors as delicately as a brain surgeon—or the camp counselor I'd once been who used two sticks and a flat rock to bisect an earthworm for baiting fishing hooks so no one would have to touch the icky worm—I opened the tiny package.

I stared at a man's head in left-facing profile on a gold disk a little bigger than a dime, and read the words "Christian IX, 1867, Konge Af Danmark." On the reverse was "20 Daler/2000 cents" beneath a delicately detailed rendition of what appeared to be a field of sugarcane waving in a gentle breeze and above that, "Dansk Vestindien." On the obverse edges were remnants of a substance that looked like candle wax.

How had such a treasure ended up in the hands of the spitter?

I picked up the phone to call Miss Maude, St. Chris's favorite retired schoolteacher and leading local historian, but hung up when I remembered she was still in Copenhagen leading a Friends of Denmark tour. I carefully wrapped the coin in a fresh tissue and slipped it into the zipper pocket of my tote for safekeeping.

By 11 A.M. Gilda's winds were up to fifty-six miles per hour, and the barometric pressure had dropped to 29.53 inches. But she was still bearing down on Tobago and no immediate threat to St. Chris.

"Gilda is much ado about *nada*," I reported to Margo at the Watering Hole round table when I begged off our Saturday night dinner. "Michael wants to get off the rock, so we're heading to St. Martin for the weekend."

"I wish Paul and I were going someplace," said Margo. "I've got a bad case of rock fever."

"You went to St. Bart's in June."

"That was then, this is now."

"I'll bring you some Dutch cheese from Phillipsburg."

"Is that a bribe? Do you want me to take care of Minx while you're gone?"

"We're only going to be away overnight. She'll be fine at home. When I get back I'll bribe her with French Friskies from the supermarket in Marigot."

"If you change your mind, drop off your keys Saturday morning and I'll go out and feed Minx."

"If you and Paul want a weekend in the country, stay at my house. The freezer's stocked, and you know where I keep the liquor."

"I may take you up on that offer. I'll talk to Paul and let you know at dinner tomorrow night. We can't let those good steaks go to waste."

After lunch I went to the library, located in the Danish-built two-story former Customs House on the green close

to Fort Frederick. The view of the harbor from the top of
the library's welcoming-arms staircase was spectacular.
The air was so clear I could see the silhouettes of the out-
islands etched on the horizon—and, if I looked hard
enough, flashes of sunlight glinting off faraway windows.
The sea was as calm as a millpond. It would be a great
time for paddling in Top Banana, but I was on a mission.

The librarian allowed me to enter the locked, private
room where the uncirculated Caribbean collection was
housed.

I scanned the shelves, then settled myself at a small
table to browse a slim volume titled *Colonial Coinage of
the Danish West Indies*, privately printed by an amateur
numismatist.

None of the coins depicted matched the one hidden in
my tote.

But a paragraph in the book's preface caught my eye,
and I copied it verbatim into my date book.

"In 1849 a new monetary system was introduced into
the Danish West Indies, replacing the former value of one
daler = 96 skilling. The Danish daler was equated with
the U.S. dollar, and divided into 100 cents. However, due
to a silver shortage during a period when the value of the
bullion was greater than the face value of coins themselves, the first coins minted under the new monetary system were not issued until 1859. The first known coins
bearing the likeness of the Danish monarch Christian IX,
crowned in 1863 upon the death of Frederik VII, were
minted by the Danish government in 1878. Rumors of an
earlier issue in 1867, purportedly lost in transit to the Danish West Indies during a catastrophic hurricane, have
proven unfounded. Many counterfeits of coins issued between 1859 and 1904 are known to exist."

As I was searching the shelves for more information on
the 1867 hurricane, the librarian tapped on the door to tell
me the library was closing for the day.

I hurried home to feed Minx, change for dinner with Michael and secrete the coin in my closet floor safe. Probably a fake, I muttered to myself, but better safe than sorry. Minx looked up from her bowl to give me one of those baleful cat stares—I refuse to believe she understood my lousy pun—then resumed eating her tuna and whitefish.

Chapter
6

I SAT ON the bench at Dockside waiting for the ferry to cross from the pier at Papaya Quay. Autotimed lights softly glowed in the lush gardens surrounding Harborview while the dining-room terrace was bathed in the golden light of the setting sun.

"It looks like a stage set from here, doesn't it, Mama?"

When had I heard Michael say those words before? I looked up, half-expecting to see him in black tie, but he was wearing freshly pressed khaki Dockers and a long-sleeved collarless white shirt. Still, the black-tie image persisted.

We held hands as we walked along the path—perfumed with the scent of night-blooming jasmine—from the Harborview pier to the dining room.

As soon as we were seated at a table on the terrace, the waiter brought a bottle of champagne and popped the cork.

Michael raised his glass. "This is where you and I had our first date."

"Our first date was a fish and chips dinner at the Lower Deck."

"Our first official date. But the first time we were out together was at Mrs. H's black-tie farewell party here at Harborview. Six months ago today." Michael reached in his pants pocket and handed me a small robin's-egg-blue box tied with a white ribbon. A box I hadn't seen since the days I used to window-shop on Michigan Avenue in Chicago. Then I realized why he'd been whistling "Moon River" when he left the station. Very sneaky. "Happy Anniversary, Mama."

"But I didn't get you anything."

"No one's keeping score, Mama. If you want to buy me something, we can shop in St. Martin this weekend. Open your present."

Inside the box was a sterling silver key ring. Hanging from the ring was a London bobby's whistle engraved with our initials and the date.

"If you ever want anything, Mama, just whistle."

"Wait! I know the rest of that line. It's Bogie and Bacall. 'You know how to whistle . . . you just put your lips together and blow.' " I held the whistle to my mouth. In Chicago a fleet of taxis would have screeched to a halt at my feet. But on the Harborview terrace, the waiter just laughed.

"Try again without the prop."

I puckered my lips and Michael leaned over to plant a soft kiss on my mouth. Over his shoulder I saw Leila Mae enter the terrace arm in arm with a man I thought was the same one she'd been with Tuesday night, but both times it was too dark to see his features clearly. I was also too far away to hear what was being said, but the conversation looked very intense. She glanced in our direction, and a curious expression crossed her face. She whispered to her companion, and they quickly left the terrace.

"A penny for your thoughts."

"I was looking at Leila Mae."

"Forget her, Mama." To his credit, Michael didn't even turn around; his blue eyes remained fixed on my face. "That was a long time ago, and this is our night." He reached across the table for my hand. "I will always be here for you."

"Well, now, isn't this precious. I just know y'all are celebrating something special." Leila Mae materialized at our table, dressed in flowing gauzy white like a digestion-induced ghost straight out of Dickens. "You must be Michael. We weren't formally introduced the other night. I'm Leila . . ." She looked down at the ring on her left hand. "How silly of me. I'm Baroness Thorsen now. But please call me Leila. And do tell me y'all are going to be at my little party Saturday night. I'll be absolutely crushed if you're not there."

Michael looked amused. "Since we don't know each other, my absence won't be a big disappointment. Kelly and I are going off-island for the weekend."

"Not you, too? Half the people I invited are going to be away." Leila Mae looked angry enough to stomp her little foot. "I have such a lovely surprise planned. You won't want to miss it."

"Don't let us spoil your fun," I said.

Michael excused himself and left the table.

Leila Mae slid into his empty chair. "Kelly, I think it's downright mean of you to spoil my party. I can't believe you're still holding a grudge over a little thing that happened five years ago."

"That little thing was an affair with my husband."

"Oh pooh. It didn't mean anything. I don't know what you're so riled about. I left the island just so you and Peter could get back together. Don't blame me if it didn't work out."

I was so angry I could have spit nails in her eyes. "I think you've overstayed your welcome. Perhaps you'd better go and change." I picked up my champagne flute and tossed its contents right into Leila Mae's smug little face.

I knew instantly I'd been a fool for letting Leila Mae get to me. Out of the corner of my eye I saw the waiter silently applauding, but I still felt mortified.

The shocked expression on Leila Mae's face quickly turned to pure hatred. "Peter always said you were a frigid bitch."

The steel band immediately began a very loud rendition of "Light My Fire."

"Mama, they're playing our song. Let's dance." Michael pulled me out of my chair onto the dance floor. When we returned to the table, Leila Mae had vanished.

After our lobster dinner we had time to stop for homemade coconut ice cream before Michael went to work. Maubi's Hot to Trot roach coach was parked in its usual spot in the waterfront parking area.

"Hey, Morning Lady. Hey, Michael. You two looking good this fine evening. What'll it be?"

Maubi, a construction worker forced into early retirement by an accident that shattered his left leg, scooped our double-dip cones while we waited for the latest weather forecast from the old boom box sitting high on a back shelf inside the van. At the 5 P.M. update Gilda's winds were still fifty-six miles per hour, the same as they'd been at 11 A.M., but the pressure had dropped. A sure sign the storm was intensifying.

"Don't need to wait for the weatherman to tell me what I already know," said Maubi. "My bum leg telling me there's a big storm coming."

"It's headed for Tobago," I said.

"My leg paining me bad." Maubi pointed to the night sky where a flock of egrets, their snowy white plumage intensified by the moonlight, headed out to sea. "The animals know for true. The old-timers used to say that you knew a storm come when the sea stay calm for many days and you see all the little fishes swim up top."

"Mama, what I know is Saturday morning we're on a plane out of here at seven sharp."

Maubi shook his head as he handed us the cones. "Michael, come Saturday morning you best be at the lumberyard buying plywood. Same as me."

Chapter
7

GILDA TURNED NORTH Friday morning.

The official report came via our first live update from the National Hurricane Center in Miami.

"At eleven o'clock Tropical Storm Gilda was located at 12.5 degrees north, 47.0 degrees west, on a west-northwest path with maximum sustained winds of sixty-three miles per hour. Further strengthening is expected, and Gilda may achieve hurricane status later today. A tropical storm watch has been posted for St. Chris and the surrounding northern Leeward Islands. Stay tuned to this radio station for the next update at 5 P.M. Atlantic Standard Time."

I began drafting a memo to all WBZE employees. A hurricane contingency plan based on ifs. *If* the storm continued north, *if* it became a hurricane, *if* a hurricane watch was posted for St. Chris . . . if, if, if. It was enough to drive a person crazy. The best I could do was plan ahead and pray Gilda gave St. Chris a pass. I should have been praying rather than playing on Hurricane Supplication

Day, one of two St. Chris official holidays devoted to hurricanes. On Supplication Day in July we pray to be spared; on Hurricane Thanksgiving in October we give thanks for having made it through the season safely.

When I took the completed memo out to Emily to distribute with the weekly paychecks, she handed me three 'urgent–call me back' phone messages. Michael, Michael and Margo.

"Mama, I heard the eleven o'clock. But I phoned the airport and everything's cool. We're still on for the weekend. Go home and pack. I'll meet you at Margo's at six for dinner."

"Kel? Are you coming to town for lunch? Bring more hurricane maps; we're running low."

Before going to town to deposit my paycheck in the bank and meet the gang at the Watering Hole, I detoured to the market to stock up on Tab. I was down to my last case. Unless I have four cases in my pantry, I worry about an impending Tab famine before the next trailer arrives on a cargo ship. The market was in its usual Friday mid-day lethargy. Shopping carts were parked in tidy rows at the entrance, the bread man was methodically stocking the racks with hot dog and hamburger buns for Labor Day weekend barbeques, the clerks at the checkout were reading magazines and chatting about party plans. Gilda was far, far away and of no more concern than a passing shower that might put a brief damper on a beach picnic.

"Kel, I've been here almost twenty years," said Jerry over lunch, "and we've never taken a direct hit. You'll see. You still going away for the weekend?"

"Michael called the airport this morning. The planes are flying, and so are we."

"Paul said there's nothing showing up yet on radar, not even a feeder band," remarked Margo. "He's got a charter booked for St. Thomas tomorrow morning. I'm going to spend a lazy Saturday at home on the beach with a trashy book."

"Why don't you come with me to Leila's party tomorrow night? Heidi doesn't want to go. You could be my date," Jerry said to Margo.

"Date, hell," said Margo, "more like your chaperone. You need a keeper, Jerry. Ask Abby."

"Ask me what?" Abby said as she put down her briefcase and slid into one of the battered captain's chairs.

"Jerry's looking for a date for Leila Mae's party. Heidi stood him up," said Margo.

"Don't look at me, Jerry," replied Abby. "I'd rather be tossed naked in a pool of piranha than go to that party."

"What is it with you women?" asked Jerry. "When did you all get so catty? So Leila screwed around a bit. It's ancient history. Get over it."

"Jerry, it wasn't your marriage that ended up on the rocks," I snapped.

"Kel, we all know the rocks are in Jerry's brain," said Margo, watching him order a fresh drink. She tapped her temple with her finger. "Poor Jerry. They say memory is the first thing to go."

"Wait up, Carole," said Jerry. He looked around the table, a placating smile on his face. "Who else wants a drink? It's on my tab."

We all accepted Jerry's unprecedented drink offer along with his unspoken apology. He gulped his drink and left to make his two o'clock tee time.

"I heard Leila Mae had a champagne bath at Harborview last night," said Abby, grinning wickedly.

I felt my face begin to redden.

"Do tell," said Margo. "What happened?"

"Someone threw a glass of champagne in her face."

"I wish it had been me," said Margo. "Whoever did it should get a medal."

"It was me," I said, "and I'm not proud of it."

"Give me a break," said Abby. "That bitch deserved it. Kel, I'm going to tell you something I've kept quiet about for five years."

"Do you want me to leave?" asked Margo.

I looked at Abby. She shrugged and said, "it's not privileged. Your call, Kel."

"Stay. You know I'd tell you later anyway."

Margo signaled Carole for another round.

"What I'm going to say stays at this table," said Abby. "Raise your glass if you agree."

We raised our glasses high.

"Kel, when you found Leila Mae in your bed with Pete—you called me at home that evening from Dockside, remember?—I went back to my office to pick up a file I needed for court the next morning. There they were, going at it on my office couch."

"Wasn't she working for you then?" asked Margo.

"Only as a temp while Barbara was on maternity leave. I fired Leila Mae on the spot. You see, I'd never given her a key to my office. She had one made behind my back."

"Jesus. What a piece of work." Margo slammed her glass on the table in disgust.

"I told Leila Mae she'd worn out her welcome and had a week to get off the island or I'd have her arrested for unlawful entry. Then I informed Pete that if you wanted a divorce, Kel, he'd better play fair on a settlement or I'd hang him out to dry."

"*Brava,* Abby! And bully for you, Kel. I'm glad you doused her. If you ever want to do it again, I'll spring for the champagne." Margo looked at her watch. "I've got to go; I need to stop at the market on the way home. Later, guys."

I turned to Abby. "Why didn't you tell me this before?"

"You were pretty beat-up emotionally, Kel. I didn't want to add to your misery."

"I'm surprised Leila Mae had the nerve to come back here," I said, signaling Carole for my bill.

"Nerve runs in the family," replied Abby. "Daddy is a convicted felon. Forgery."

"Really? How interesting. What did he forge?" I asked. "Monet rip-offs? Phony Rembrandts?"

"Stock certificates and banknotes. I also heard he was involved in a couple of Ponzi schemes. Leila Mae and Daddy are a pair of snakes," said Abby, reaching for her briefcase. "Don't ever turn your back on either one of them. It cost me a lot to learn that lesson."

It was after three when I finally headed home to pack for the weekend.

The five o'clock update was in progress when I hopped out of the shower. Gilda's winds were up to sixty-nine miles per hour, but the maximum forward speed had decreased. The latest prediction put St. Chris and the northern Leewards in the clear for the weekend.

Michael and I sat with Margo and Paul on their gallery at Sea Breezes watching the sunset paint a sky that looked like a kid had been let loose with jars of luminescent finger paints.

"Honey, when the steaks are on the grill, I'll put the potatoes in the microwave and make béarnaise sauce. I do it in a blender—if it works for Julia Child, it works for me," said Margo. "Kel brought a key lime pie for dessert."

Michael visibly salivated. "Did you make it yourself, Mama? If so, I'll skip dinner and start with dessert."

"If there are any crumbs left in the pan, you can take them to the station for a midnight snack," said Margo.

We ate on the gallery under a canopy of stars, watching Scorpio move across the sky. A pleasant evening of good food shared with good friends. If I'd been Minx, I would have licked my paws and purred.

Michael was already into his show when I thanked Margo and Paul for a great time.

"Kel, drop off your house keys when you pick up Michael in the morning. I'll run out and feed Minx."

"Are you sure?"

"No problem, sweetie; I'll be around all weekend."

At 11 P.M. Gilda was upgraded to a category one hurricane. But her forward motion was slowing to a crawl, and she was still far from land. I went to sleep dreaming of Michael's naked body on a sugar sand beach.

Chapter
8

MY WEEKEND PLANS were blown out of the water by a phone call at four-forty-five Saturday morning.

"Mama, grab your Tab. I've got bad news and not-so-bad news. You choose."

"Easy. Not-so-bad."

"You're going to the airport at six, and I'm going with you."

"I already knew that. Now give me the bad."

"Margo and Paul are going with us."

"To St. Martin? What's so bad about that?"

"You haven't heard the really bad part. They're going to Bonaire, and we're staying home because our flight's been canceled. The latest update from Miami says Gilda's up to eighty-one miles per hour and heading for us at warp speed like a bitch on a broomstick. Paul has to get his plane out of here before the weather turns."

"Damn. I'm sorry, Michael. I know how much you wanted to get away this weekend."

"I'm bummed out about it. I kept thinking about you on that nude beach."

"I had a dream about it myself last night. Tell you what, we'll try again for next weekend. Do I need to call Margo?"

"No, she's expecting us. Have you got any coffee? I need a java fix."

"I'll bring a Thermos with me. See you in thirty."

I waited for the five o'clock update before leaving my house. Gilda was only a category one hurricane but expected to intensify as she traveled over the unseasonably warm Caribbean waters. She was still more than a day away from St. Chris. A hurricane watch had been posted for all of the northern Leeward Islands, to be upgraded to a hurricane warning when Gilda was twenty-four hours from impact.

The sky reflected in my rearview mirror was flashed with pink as I drove along the deserted east-end road toward Isabeya. I envied the residents slumbering peacefully in their beds, unaware of Gilda's latest position. I saw a flock of pelicans soaring and swooping into the placid sea, glanced at a countryside glowing with multihued hibiscus and remnants of orange and red flamboyant blazing against verdant hillsides. Sugar birds twittered in their nests, while hummingbirds flitted from flower to flower, slurping nectar.

I reached the outskirts of Isabeya without seeing another car. When I parked in my reserved spot in the station parking area, Michael was standing at the studio window panting like a camel nearing an oasis. I picked up the Thermos and a bag of chocolate chip cookies and hightailed it into the station.

"Change of plan, Mama," Michael mumbled, as he alternately slurped and munched, while I scrawled a hurricane schedule for the weekend part-time staff on a chalkboard.

"Now what?" I called over my shoulder as I propped the board in the reception area where everyone would see it when they reported for work. For the 6 A.M. Saturday to 6 A.M. Monday weekend, WBZE is staffed by four part-time deejays, rotating in six-hour shifts. During the week, Michael and I and two other disk jockeys fill the local airwaves with music, chat, news and weather.

Michael followed behind me, devouring the last cookie. "You're taking Margo and Paul to the airport, I'm going home on my bike. Pick me up after you've dropped them at the hangar and we'll head for the lumberyard. I've got some boarding up to do if I'm going to ride out the storm with you on the air."

"You don't have to be here. It's not your responsibility. Take the weekend off and lime."

"Where are you going to be?"

"Here at the station. From Sunday noon on. Didn't you read my Friday memo? It was in the envelope with your paycheck."

"I was supposed to read it? I made a paper airplane out of it." Michael smiled. "Mama, where you go, I go. That's how it is with us. Don't you know that yet?" He hugged me, leaving a trail of cookie crumbs on my chin. "Go. Margo and Paul are waiting for you. See you at my place."

My unflappable friend Margo had completely lost her cool.

"Kel, this is totally nuts. I've been up since four packing, trying to get this place closed up. I don't know what I'm doing. Paul, where did I put my purse?"

"Honey, it's on the chair behind you, and I've got your passport in my briefcase. Why don't you chill out for a minute while I take the luggage downstairs. Where did you park, Kel?"

"Out in front. Everything's unlocked, including the hatch."

Paul headed down the outside stairs toward the parking lot, loaded like a Sherpa.

"I forgot to make the bed." Margo ran toward the bed-room.

I called after her, "Margo, let it go. It's not important."

"It is to me."

Paul came back for a second load. "Where's Margo?"

"Making the bed."

Paul smiled. "Kel, would you mind checking the kitchen? Make sure the coffeepot's turned off?"

I unplugged the coffeepot, dumped the grounds in the garbage bin and rinsed the glass carafe, leaving it upside down to drip-dry in the sink. I picked up the plastic trash bag, full of scraps and bones from our steak dinner, and took it to the front door. I'd drop the trash at the dump on the way to the airport.

"The coffeepot. I forgot to turn off the coffeepot."

"It's done, Margo. I took care of it."

"Thanks, Kel. I don't know where my head's at this morning." She looked around her living room. "Where's Michael?"

"He's going home on his bike. After I drop you, we're off to the lumberyard for plywood."

"Are you going to be all right? I hate going away and leaving everyone behind."

"Margo, don't worry about it. I'll be fine. Michael and I are going to ride out the storm at the station. By next weekend, you and I'll be sitting on the beach sipping piña coladas like nothing ever happened."

Paul picked Margo's purse off the chair and handed it to her. "Honey, we've got to go. I have to get the plane fueled and file a flight plan. Why don't you and Kel wait at the car, while I close the hurricane shutters and lock the sliding glass doors. I'll be down in five minutes."

Margo and I stood at my car, listening to the morning breeze tickle the fronds on the palm trees lining the Sea Breezes parking area. The clattering fronds echoed the tapping of Margo's fingernails on the roof of my hatch-back.

"I know I'm forgetting something," said Margo, peering into her oversize shoulder bag. "My book. I forgot my book." She ran for the stairs and collided with Paul coming down with his briefcase and a thick paperback book he handed to Margo with a broad smile. She threw her arms around him and kissed him with a passion usually reserved for a late-late show on the soft-porn channel.

I busied myself closing the hatch and said a silent thank-you to Michael for volunteering to stick with me at the station. Margo had said early in my relationship with Michael that, like Paul, he was a guy I could trust. I remembered her saying "when I met Paul I knew I could put my life in his hands and he wouldn't drop it."

After Margo wiped a faint smudge of lipstick from Paul's mouth, they settled themselves in my car, grinning like teenage lovers.

Traffic was still sparse. When we reached the airport turnoff I had the road to myself.

The St. Chris International Airport—a fancy name for a tin-roofed one-story structure with only two gates—is located on the west end near the south shore and boasts a great sea view and a very popular free rum bar at baggage claim.

A lone taxi van was disgorging a family with a mound of luggage and two cranky children for the morning's first outbound commercial flight when I drove past the main entrance to the narrower side road leading to the area where private planes were parked.

Paul disappeared inside the hangar and returned with an empty baggage cart. "The plane's being fueled now. If you two will load the cart, I'll get my flight plan filed."

"Kel, I don't know why we're leaving so soon," said Margo, plopping the last duffel bag on the cart. "I thought the airport would be mobbed, but there's no one here. I feel like we're running away from nothing. Have you ever seen such a beautiful morning?"

"By this afternoon you'll be relaxing on a sunny beach in Bonaire," I said. "A free vacation is a hell of a lot cheaper than a wrecked plane."

"I suppose so," said Margo with a sigh. "Kel, take my keys. If you need anything in the condo, help yourself. My car key's there too. You've got my cell-phone number? Call me. Here, take my phone. You may need it."

I reached in my own tote for my cell-phone case. "I bought one on Wednesday."

Margo laughed for the first time that morning. "I knew you had a list." She threw her arms around me in a big hug. "Take care of yourself, sweetie. I'll miss you."

"Me too," I said, forcing a smile to check any tears that might be lurking. "Keep your hands off the pilot until you're safe on the ground."

"Let's go, honey. I've got clearance and want to get out of here before the big jet's ready to depart."

I stood at the hangar, waving good-bye to my best friends. Paul waggled the wings after takeoff as the plane gently turned toward the south.

Chapter
9

WHEN THE DOORS opened at eight, there were more employees than customers at the lumberyard.

One of the first faces I saw was Benjamin's eight-year-old son Trevor.

"Did you know there's a hurricane coming?" said Trevor, bouncing with excitement. "Its name is Gilda. Isn't that a silly name? It sounds like a witch in *The Wizard of Oz*. Have you ever seen *The Wizard of Oz*? My mom bought me the video. Miss Kelly, you could come to our house sometime and watch it with me."

"Trevor, it's okay if you call me Kelly."

"Oh, I can't do that," said Trevor.

"Why not?"

"Well, my mom said—" Trevor stopped squirming to stand perfectly still. He looked at me with his head cocked like an inquisitive bird, reminding me of a parakeet I once owned named Sasha.

"If it's not a secret, you can tell me. What did your mother say?"

"My mom said I should respect old people. Are you older than my mom? She's thirty-two. I know because I looked at her passport."

Out of the mouths of babes. "Yes, Trevor, I'm older than your mother." At that moment I also felt older than dirt.

"But you're not as old as Miss Maude, are you? She's coming back from Denmark this afternoon. She said she'd bring me some Danish stamps for my collection. I'm starting third grade next week."

"I didn't know you collected stamps."

"I collect coins, too. But my mom said it's not nice to ask people for money."

"Where is your mother? You're not here by yourself, are you?"

"She's at the high school, getting the windows boarded up. My dad's out back buying plywood. What are you buying? I'm supposed to be looking for batteries. My dad says we need lots and lots."

"I think the batteries are over here," I said, taking Trevor by the hand.

Benjamin and Michael found us filling a small shopping basket with batteries of all sizes.

"Hey, Trevor, how's the volleyball coming?" asked Michael.

"Hi, Michael," said Trevor. "I heard you on the radio this morning talking about the storm. I wanted to play volleyball this weekend at the beach, but my dad said we have to take care of the house first. Dad, look at this flashlight; it's really neat. Can I have one of these for my room?"

Benjamin added a baby SnakeLight and extra AA batteries to the basket, then sent Trevor to the checkout.

"Gilda could be bad, Kelly," said Benjamin. He stood looking around the deserted store. "I wish more people were taking this seriously. I don't have the manpower to be out rescuing people who didn't take care of themselves. If this thing is really headed our way, we're going to have to put a curfew in place tomorrow. I was told an hour ago there's an emergency meeting at Government House this afternoon at three-thirty. You should be there."

"I was told there might be a meeting, but I didn't know it was definite," I said. "I've already put my staff on hurricane leave beginning tomorrow at noon."

"Most of my police officers will also be on leave," replied Benjamin. "But I'll be on duty at the station."

"That makes two of us," I said, smiling. Michael cleared his throat. "Make that three. Michael's going to be on the air with me." We walked toward the checkout. "Trevor said Miss Maude's coming home today from Denmark."

"Her plane gets in from Miami midafternoon," Benjamin replied. "It may be the last inbound flight. Camille and Amelia will be picking her up at the airport to take her home when they're through with storm preparations at the school."

Benjamin's wife Camille was the assistant principal to Miss Maude's granddaughter Amelia, the principal of the island's only public high school.

"Tell Camille I'll call Miss Maude later to see if there's anything she needs," I said to Benjamin. "I'll see you this afternoon at Government House."

"I think you and I will be seeing a lot of each other in the next few days," said Benjamin with a wry smile.

"Michael, I tell you for true I see you here today," Maubi called out as he entered the front door. I noticed Maubi was using his cane and knew his leg was bothering him.

We all wished each other safe passage through the storm and continued on our errands.

By 11 A.M. Gilda's winds were up to ninety-two miles per hour.

I spent the late morning and early afternoon at home boxing supplies to take to the station, between doing loads of laundry and trying to decide where I'd stash the furniture and plants from my screened-in gallery, where twelve sets of Woodstock wind chimes hung mute in the sultry air.

Minx paced the length of my small home, formerly a Danish one-room schoolhouse, unable to settle herself in one spot for more than a minute. She followed on my heels with small questioning cries. When I picked her up to comfort her, she squirmed from my grasp and refused to be placated with her favorite Haute Feline kitty treats.

Shortly before three I tossed a large cooler in my car, to fill with bags of ice from the market after the meeting at Government House, and headed back to Isabeya.

The narrow one-way streets of Isabeya were clogged with cars passing through town, but the sidewalks were devoid of foot traffic. The duty-free perfume, liquor and imported clothing shops had closed at noon for the long Labor Day holiday weekend.

I parked in the empty lot next to Fort Frederick and walked across the green to Government House.

In 1764, most of the buildings in Isabeya were destroyed by a catastrophic town fire. The first phase of new three-story Government House, relocated at the foot of Kongens Gade across from the fort and the library, was completed by the Danes five years later, and some say construction has never ceased.

Government House has always been a work in progress as various areas are continually being expanded or remodeled and the exterior coral-and-molasses walls—the tropical equivalent of Elizabethan wattle and daub—are repainted annually in historic mustard yellow. The building complex is accented with forest green shutters and topped with a bright red roof.

Besides serving as the governor's residence, Govern-

ment House is also the address of various government
offices, including the court and recorder of deeds. On the
second floor is a magnificent ballroom—with original furnishings transported from Denmark by sailing ship, including teak and mahogany parquet floors and
hand-blown glass globes on gaslight fixtures—where for-
mal government functions from bill signings to inaugural
balls have been held since 1769.

We were meeting in a ground-floor room, once part of
the horse stables, at the rear of the Government House
complex. The sound of water splashing in the courtyard
fountain made me wish I'd stopped at the loo before the
meeting began.

In attendance were representatives from the power
plant, telephone company, fire and police departments
and, representing the department of education, my nemesis from the Navidad de Isabeya parade committee, Mr.
Daniel.

The meeting was chaired by Chris, the governor's aide.
"The governor regrets he cannot be present this afternoon,
but he is preoccupied with other matters," he said, as he
opened the meeting.

I felt a subtle nudge from Benjamin and tried not to
look his way or smile. It was no secret that the governor
was overly fond of our leading export, 151-proof rum. If
he wasn't nursing a hangover at that particular moment,
the governor was probably well on his way to another
one.

We were dealing with a contingency plan based on ifs.
If the storm intensified past a category one, *if* a hurricane
warning was posted for St. Chris, *if* Gilda was predicted
to directly impact our island. Then the airport would be
closed to all traffic, a curfew would be in effect until the
storm passed, and power would be shut off islandwide.
But no one could predict when these events would occur.
Or if.

Mr. Daniel took the floor. "Speaking for the school-children, I am most distressed by this unfortunate turn of events. Our schools are scheduled to open, as is our custom, on Tuesday, the day after Labor Day. If there is no power available, I cannot require the children to be present and makeup days will have to be added to the end of the term, curtailing the long-anticipated Christmas break. When I am elected to the Senate this fall . . ."

Self-serving rhetoric always triggers my gag reflex. I quickly excused myself to make a pit stop at the loo. On the way back to the meeting room, I used my new cell phone to call WBZE for the latest weather update. The five o'clock advisory had just come over the Teletype from Miami.

"Gentlemen, I think we can drop the ifs and proceed to when," I said, reentering the meeting room. "I just got off the phone with the station, and here's the latest update. Gilda is now a category two hurricane with winds of ninety-eight miles per hour. A hurricane warning has been posted for all of the northern Leewards. Her forward motion has decreased, which means the storm is intensifying. At her current speed, she's expected to hit St. Chris sometime tomorrow evening."

I addressed my final remarks to Mr. Daniel. "I wouldn't gas up the school buses just yet; I don't think the children will be going back to school on Tuesday."

Chapter
10

THE SUPERMARKET WAS jammed with shoppers competing in a "who can stuff the most in a cart in five minutes and get to the checkout first" buying frenzy. Checkout lines snaked through the aisles all the way back to the meat department. I waited my turn in line by reading one of the trashy tabloids—a cover story titled "Alien Baby Fathered by Elvis?" was a real time killer—but when I finally inched my way to the cashier, the ice machine was empty.

I ran out to the parking lot, using my cell phone to call Soup to Nuts, a gourmet deli on the east end of town and my biggest advertiser. They were about to close, but would wait if I could get there in ten minutes or less. I placed an order to go, begged the loan of a wicker picnic basket and jumped in my car, feeling like a driver at Indy when the race official yells "gentlemen, start your engines."

Michael was leaning against his Harley when I pulled into my driveway at five-forty-five.

"Get in the car," I said. "You're being abducted."

I drove down to the secluded cove where Top Banana, my bright yellow Ocean Scrambler kayak, was chained to a palm tree.

"It's not Orient Bay, but it'll have to do," I said, smiling as I shed my shorts and T-shirt. Michael was quick on the uptake and soon we were cavorting in the tepid Caribbean Sea like a pair of baby dolphins.

We swam toward the reef a quarter mile out, feeling the slap of rising easterly swells against our backs. Halfway to the reef, we stopped to tread water and watch the fireball sun sink into the sea with an inaudible sizzle. While the vivid sky colors faded to gray, we stroked against the current back to the cove.

What no one ever mentions about the *From Here to Eternity* beach scene is how much the sand itches and how it scrapes against parts of your body, places where sand was never meant to be. I sang alternative lyrics to "What I Did for Love" from *A Chorus Line*—my version began with "kiss your ass good-bye"—while Michael and I wrestled Top Banana into the hatch of my car and stabilized it between the full ice chest and now empty picnic basket for the short trip home.

Minx greeted me with "do I know you?" glares and yowls, thoroughly annoyed that I hadn't stopped to feed her before heading down to the beach, but was somewhat mollified when Michael put the last of the goose liver pâté into her food dish.

"Mama, where in the hell are you going to put all that stuff?"

"All what stuff?"

"That stuff." He pointed to the gallery. "You've got another houseful of furniture sitting out there."

"Never you mind, I worked it all out."

"Lay it on me. This house is like one of those sliding

puzzles. Every time you move something, something else has to go in a different spot."

"The plants will go in the shower, the gallery furniture will go on top of the bed and the chimes will get boxed in empty Tab cartons and stashed under the bed. Satisfied, smart-ass?"

"What about the roll-down blinds?"

I'd forgotten about those.

"There's room under the bed."

"And the kayak?"

"Behind the living-room couch. But not until tomorrow morning or we'll be tripping over it all evening."

Michael and I went to sleep after the eleven o'clock update. Gilda's winds had increased to 104 miles per hour. Her forward speed put her only sixteen hours away from St. Chris.

Chapter

11

We woke Sunday morning to the next update from the National Hurricane Center in Miami.

"At 5 A.M., Gilda was upgraded to a category three hurricane with maximum sustained winds of 115 miles per hour. She is still on a west-northwest course and residents of the northern Leewards will begin feeling its effects by midafternoon. On the current track, the eye of this well-defined storm will pass over St. Chris later this evening. Final storm preparations should be in place by noon."

I immediately called Benjamin at home. Camille answered the phone in a whisper.

"Camille, is everything all right?" I whispered back.

"Ben is still sleeping, and I don't want to wake him. This may be the last good night's sleep he'll have for a few days."

"Ask him to call me at home later. Did Miss Maude get back all right?"

"She's fine. I gave her your message, and she sends her

love. She'll be in touch with you after the storm."

"Does she need anything? Is there anything I can do for her?"

"Amelia and her husband are going over to Miss Maude's this morning to help her secure the house. I took her grocery shopping yesterday on the way home from the airport. Oh, now Trevor's awake. Kelly, I've really got to go. Ben will call you."

I went to the kitchen to start coffee for Michael and pop a cold Tab for myself. Minx sat next to her empty food bowl, tail twitching like a metronome.

"What was all that whispering about, Mama? Secrets?"

"Hardly. Benjamin's still sleeping, and Camille didn't want to wake him. Make your coffee while I feed Minx."

We stood on the gallery looking at a sky as brilliantly colored as the hibiscus blooming throughout the valley. The normal pastoral morning sound of chirping sugar birds and noisily crowing roosters was quickly displaced by a cacophony of incessant hammering, electric drills sounding like a thousand dentists in a marathon cavity-filling contest and the r-r-u-u-p-p of gas-powered generators being tested.

Michael helped haul the gallery furnishings into the house and secure plywood over the sliding glass doors and adjacent jalousie windows. The rest of the windows had permanently installed wooden hurricane shutters I could easily close and bolt myself.

Benjamin called before eight to report that the airport would be closed to commercial traffic at ten, after the morning flight departed for San Juan, and a curfew would be in place islandwide beginning at 3 P.M. to keep the roads clear for emergency vehicles.

"The power plant will stay on-line as long as possible. There is still a faint chance that the storm may turn more to the north. The cable station will begin shutting down its satellite dishes, but will keep the Weather Channel on the air as long as there is power. I'll drop off an emergency pass for you at the station so you won't be stopped on the roads."

Michael left to finish his own storm prep, saying he'd see me at the station before curfew. I called WBZE to relay Benjamin's advisories and told Rick to keep broadcasting the storm news every fifteen minutes until I was there to relieve him at noon. The second I put down the phone it rang.

"Where's Margo? I've been calling her all morning."

"Top of the morning, Jerry. Margo and Paul split early yesterday for Bonaire. Paul had to get the plane out of here. What's up? How was the party?"

"God-awful, Kel. Can you believe there was a cash bar?"

I burst out laughing. "How was the food?"

"Cheap. Just those veggie things with dip and some dried-up cheese on soggy crackers. I had to go home to get something decent to eat. I spent more time putting on my tux than I did at the party."

"Did you at least get to meet Christian?"

"Leila said he was on the phone. International conference call. I never laid eyes on him."

"What was Leila Mae's big surprise?"

"What surprise?"

"She told me she was going to make an announcement at the party. Something no one should miss."

"I was too thirsty to stick around long enough to hear the news. I'll nose around this morning. Where are you going to be?"

"Home in the morning, at the station from noon on."

"I'll get back to you, Kel. Stop by my house for a Bloody if you've got time."

I caught Minx trying to sneak outside while I was hauling Top Banana through the kitchen door. I was afraid she'd head off on safari and I'd never find her when it was time to leave, so I tucked her in her wicker carrier for safety. She soon discovered the catnip I'd liberally sprinkled on the bath-towel liner, and her angry yowls softened to contented purrs.

When Top Banana was dry-docked behind the couch, I rolled my hand-woven Turkish and Egyptian silk rugs and wrapped them in plastic. So much for the inside work.

I dragged the ladder outside to close and bolt the hurricane shutters. By the time I finished my task, the seed pods on the Mother Tongue trees were rattling in the freshening breeze. I looked overhead to see streamers of clouds approaching from the east; the peacock ocean was frothed with whitecapped waves racing in orderly precision, row after row after row, to the west. Ominous heralds of the approaching wrath of Gilda. The air was heavy, humid and laced with the pungent smell of salt. Or so I thought until I realized I was dripping wet with sweat. Ten-thirty. I barely had time for a quick shower before I moved the plants into the shower stall and left for town.

Everything I needed for the next couple of days, including Minx, was loaded in the car when the eleven o'clock advisory was broadcast from Miami.

"Gilda remains a category three hurricane with highest sustained winds now reaching 127 miles per hour. Her forward speed has decreased considerably and the storm appears to be building toward a category four."

I took one last look at my little house. The back and sides were somewhat protected by the east-end hills, but the front would be vulnerable to westerly winds if Gilda passed directly to the north. All I could do now was pray.

Chapter
12

I PICKED UP a copy of the *Coconut Telegraph*—dated Monday, sold Sunday, printed Saturday, containing Friday's news—when I stopped at Soup to Nuts to return the picnic basket.

The front page screamed "Gilda Takes Aim on St. Chris!" in a banner headline over a half-page hurricane map embellished with the storm track. The *Telegraph* staffers must have worked overtime because the latest position reported was 5 P.M. Saturday, the hour when the paper normally went to press. A dotted line indicating the projected path looked like a tracer bullet whizzing straight across our thirty-five-square-mile crescent-shaped island.

The narrow one-way streets in and out of Isabeya were clogged with residents scurrying to the lumberyard and supermarket and back home again before curfew.

Shop owners had taken all the parking spots in town and were busy closing hurricane shutters, nailing plywood over windows and piling sandbags in front of locked doors in meager defense against the anticipated storm surge.

In the harbor, boats pulled anchor to head for sanctuary in the Columbus Bay hurricane hole or double-anchored at permanent moorings to ride out the storm. Supply-laden dinghies zipped back and forth from the Dockside board-walk like dragonflies in heat. Novice sailors clamored for parallel docking against the security of the wharf, an easy jump to terra firma.

I downshifted to second to head up the hill toward Jerry's house on Bjer Gade. I parked on the street, block-ing his short driveway. Minx whined uneasily in her car-rier.

"Five minutes, Minx. Give me five minutes and we'll be on the way to the station; then you can get out and stretch your legs." Minx hunched sphinxlike with her head pulled into her shoulders like a turtle, glaring at me with slit eyes through the mesh door of the carrier.

Jerry called out through a front window. "Back door's open, come on in. Make yourself a drink—everything's on the kitchen counter."

I slipped through the narrow opening in the high wooden gates separating Jerry's driveway from his yard, walked around to the back of the house and entered through the kitchen as instructed. I really wanted a Bloody, but didn't have time to sit and drink it.

Jerry handed me a large Styrofoam cup and a plastic lid. "Here's a traveler, Kel. You can take it with you to finish at the station."

"I'm going to have to take a rain check on the drink; I'm really running late."

I followed Jerry to the front gallery, where sections of the Sunday New York Times lay scattered on the stone floor like autumn leaves. The gallery view was panoramic and encompassed most of Isabeya, the harbor and Papaya Quay. Jerry liked to boast that on a clear day he could see Miami through his binoculars. I noticed that the Lower

Deck at Dockside was already stripped of its tables and chairs.

"Where's Heidi?"

"In the shower. She'll be out in a minute. Sit down for a sec—I've got dirt."

I perched on the edge of a chaise. "I'm running late, Jer. Dish."

"The rumor mill says Leila's big surprise was a pitch for investors to hunt up a treasure ship that ran aground near here."

"You have got to be kidding. She came back here to con the locals? Why am I not surprised? When she lived here last time she didn't have a pot to piss in and she left bar tabs all over town. Who would give her one red cent?"

"I hear she's got maps and the ship captain's diary. And she hired some guy who found the original manifest. The ship was carrying a fortune in gold coins. This sounds like a real deal, Kel."

"Jerry, are you loose? A treasure hunt is the oldest scam in the world. Tell me you're not thinking of investing."

"It's only five hundred bucks a share, Kel. And a chance to be the next Mel Fisher."

"And what else do you get besides a boot in the bum when you kick yourself for being a sucker?"

Jerry shrugged. "I didn't get all the details."

I looked at my watch. "Jer, I've got to go this very second. Rick's waiting for me to relieve him. If I'm late, he's into overtime."

Jerry walked me to the kitchen door.

"You've got a bird's-eye view of town. Check in with me from time to time and let me know what's happening. Thanks for the drink offer and the dirt."

"Don't mention it. Call me if you need anything. Stay safe, Kel."

I stood on tiptoe to kiss his cheek. "You, too, Jerry. Will you be okay? Have you got hurricane shutters?"

"They're stacked in the back shed. I'll get to that later. The storm won't be here for hours."

Rick had already left, and Michael was on the air when I pulled into WBZE at fifteen minutes before pumpkin time.

"I haven't been home yet, Mama. Rick had to split and help his parents board up. As soon as you've unloaded your car, I'm heading out to forage for food."

"I've got a cooler full of sandwich makings."

"Let's keep those for later. I've got a feeling we're in for a long night."

I settled Minx in a corner of the studio with her litter box and food dishes.

The three incoming phone lines rang nonstop. Residents wanting to know the latest position of the storm and how long stores were open. Was it too late to get an order of propane delivered? Were the shelters open? Were gas stations still open? The three I'd passed on the way to WBZE were closed, signs on the pumps saying "Out of Gas." I played the latest taped message from Government House, announcing the curfew beginning at three and wishing all godspeed. A few tourists called for outgoing flight schedules. I hated having to tell them the last flight had left and the airport was closed to further air traffic until after the storm had passed.

"At 11 A.M., the center of Gilda was 144 miles east-southeast of St. Chris. Winds have increased to 127 miles per hour. The stores will close promptly at two and curfew begins at three. Island Lumber is out of plywood, but has some batteries and tarps left. Super Foods still has bottled water and reminds you to care for your pets."

Minx yawned broadly like the MGM icon, stretched, turned a half circle and went back to sleep.

Through the studio picture window I watched the weather deteriorate. The white wisps that streaked the sky at dawn were gone; the sky was gray, filled with churning

clouds. A steady stream of cars passed in front of the
studio. A few had turned on their lights, but there was
still no reason to use windshield wipers. The leaf-laden
limbs on the trees were beginning to sway in the gusting
winds.

The first squall hit at one-thirty with an intensity that
made me leap away from the window. Even though the
safety glass was covered outside with security ironwork,
I felt vulnerable and exposed. Treetops shook in the wind,
and torrents of rain flooded the shallow guts leading to
the sea. After a few minutes the rain decreased to a drizzle, but the winds continued to blow in ever-increasing
gusts. It was like watching someone blow up a balloon:
whoosh, who-osh, wh-oo-sh, wh-o-o-sh.

The next call was from the power plant telling me they
were shutting down at four.

"We've just had an intermediate advisory from the Hurricane Center in Miami. At 2 P.M. the center of Gilda was
one hundred miles east-southeast of St. Chris. Winds are
now clocked at 130 miles per hour, one mile short of a
category four. Hurricane-force winds extend thirty miles
from the center; tropical-storm-force winds extend sixty
miles out. If you need to get to a shelter, go now. All
stores are closed, curfew begins in less than an hour.
Power will be shut off islandwide in less than two hours."

I repeated the two o'clock position, then grabbed a
fresh Tab from the large cooler I'd packed that morning.
The duffel bag at my feet held hurricane supplies: extra
toilet paper, flashlights and batteries, clean clothes, canned
food and catnip for Minx.

Michael blew back into the studio at two-thirty smelling
of soap and shampoo, wearing one of his more garish
Polynesian shirts over cutoff jeans under a hooded yellow
slicker. On his auburn hair was his prized winged-warrior
cap, golden wings glistening with rain. The comparison

to one of the winged monkeys from The *Wizard of Oz* was too obvious to be ignored.

I made flapping motions with my hands. "You look like Margaret Hamilton's advance man."

"Hey, Lady Munchkin, your eyes are yellower than the brick road. Make a pit stop, Mama, and wash your hands for lunch." He held a large McDonald's bag aloft. "Here's the last hot meal we may see for awhile. I stashed a bucket of Kentucky Fried and some sides of potato salad and coleslaw in the refrigerator earlier this morning. We can eat that cold for dinner."

Minx bounded out of the carrier, her pepper-freckled pink nose quivering at the scent of food. "Felinus, I got the last fishy-wich for you. Come on, calico, let's put this in your bowl." Michael carefully separated the fish from the bun, breaking the patty into small pieces. Minx purred as she ran to her feast. Handel's *Water Music* filled the airwaves as we ate.

Michael handed me an ice-cold Heineken from his stash in the refrigerator.

To everyone on St. Chris the next advisory was self-evident. "At 5 P.M. Gilda was a category four with winds of 144 miles per hour. The center was located seventy-one miles east-southeast of St. Chris. The eye of Gilda should pass over the island in about five hours. We'll be feeling the full impact of the storm in the next couple of hours."

Outside, the trees were whipping from side to side like drunken apache dancers in a Left Bank Paris bistro. The wind had a frenzy and persona of its own. Like a vengeful harpy it shrieked unendingly and tore with powerful, grasping claws at everything it touched. The air was filled with leaves and tree limbs, power lines cracked against the pavement like bullwhips, street signs sliced through the air like boomerangs, pieces of galvanized roofing twisted into origami shapes by a clumsy giant sailed upward, then crashed to the ground. The rain blasted St. Chris in hard-driven sheets that appeared horizontal rather than vertical.

The hours were filled with wind, rain, and unremitting noise. God-awful clanging, banging, crashing, moaning, howling, ear-shattering, sanity-destroying noise. Noise that penetrated even the sound-proofed studio where Michael and I maintained a continual hand-holding call-in link with our listeners.

It was like broadcasting from a dimly lit sauna. We used the generator only to stay on the air. Battery-operated emergency lights gave the studio a ghostly ambience, and the air conditioners were rendered impotent when the power was cut at four.

By 8 P.M. all hell was breaking loose. Gilda's winds were up to 153 miles per hour, almost a category five. But the worst was yet to come as the eye wall approached St. Chris.

"At 11 P.M. Gilda was classified a category five hurricane with maximum sustained winds of 161 miles per hour. The center of Gilda is moving away from St. Chris to the northwest at twelve miles per hour."

That announcement was good news/bad news. Good news that the center had passed St. Chris sometime between the 8 P.M. and 11 P.M. advisories and we were on the downhill side; bad news that at the current movement we still had another four or five hours to go.

Our first caller after the eleven o'clock update told us how wrong the weather service could be. "I don't know who dreamed up that position, but they're full of crap. The eye's almost at my house on the east end now. The wind's been dropping steadily for the past ten minutes."

We warned our listeners about the approaching eye, reminding them that the dying winds didn't mean the storm was over. After the eye passed, the winds would be back full force—like a car accelerating from zip to one-sixty in twenty seconds or less—from the opposite direction. Our east-end caller reported the eye lasted almost twenty minutes at his house. Already the winds at the studio had lessened to mere puffs.

Minx cried out in pain from the change in atmospheric pressure and could not be comforted. I locked her in the carrier to keep her from running outside when I went to tend the generator.

Michael decided to check the transmitter tower.

"Are you out of your bloody mind?" I yelled, wanting to shake some sense into him. "You'll never get there and back in twenty minutes."

"I'll be back before you can say 'there's no place like home.' Give me your keys, Mama. I need to use your car."

He grabbed the new key ring he'd given me three nights earlier at our anniversary dinner at Harborview. "Where's your cell phone, Mama? I'll call you from the tower."

"Get your butt back here fast, Michael. This is really stupid. I don't like it one damned bit."

The next sound I heard was my car door slamming. The tower was two miles away, on the east side of Isabeya—a five-minute ride through town in good weather and no traffic. Who knew if the roads were still passable?

I spent the eye time tending the generator, listening every minute for the sound of my car returning. Standing on the stoop outside the front door in a night as dark and still as the inside of a pocket, I gulped fresh air that smelled like the silk from a newly shucked ear of sweet corn. Overhead tiny stars twinkled, but within seconds they were eclipsed by clouds, and the eerie stillness shattered by the returning winds.

There was still no sign of Michael.

Chapter
13

I CLOSED THE outside carved wood door. The eye had lasted only fifteen minutes. I hurried back into the studio to answer the phone. The line was full of static, and it was hard to hear Michael, even though he shouted over the wind.

"At the tower. Listing but okay. Roads a mess. Keep the front door unlocked for me . . ." I heard a crash, and the phone went dead. I tried calling back, but there was no answer.

The next few hours were a journey through hell. The westerly winds tore at the unbolted outer door, shaking it in its hinges. If I locked it, Michael would be trapped outside when he returned. Water began pouring under the door, threatening to flood the reception area. I closed the glass-paned inner door, throwing chair cushions against it to dam the water. The studio door remained open for ventilation. Minx yowled to be let out of her carrier.

The phones kept ringing with reports from people huddled in bathrooms and closets after losing their roofs, tales of boats smashed to driftwood against the dock, downed power lines and telephone poles. Long-distance service was gone. We'd lost all contact with the National Hurricane Center in Miami. The number of calls dropped steadily as broken telephone poles curtailed service. I kept trying to call Michael, punching redial/redial/redial until my finger blistered. When I tried calling the police all I heard was a continuous busy signal.

I released Minx from her prison and she leapt to the console, where she hunched within petting distance, rubbing her face and head against my hand. When I tried to leave for the loo she flew at me with bared claws. I was trapped in the studio by Minx, the water invading the reception area and the hurricane-force winds tearing at the front door. I felt like a sitting duck. In desperation I used Minx's litter box to pee, carefully shaking the box to freshen it.

The telephone pole next to the station crashed to the ground in a tangle of wires with a thud that jolted my raw-edged nerves.

The battery-powered emergency lights slowly dimmed, then died, leaving the studio in darkness. I fumbled in my duffel for flashlights and aimed the beams at the ceiling for ambient light. The winds continued to gust, appearing against all sensibility to strengthen rather than diminish.

I knew we were still on the air, although the signal was growing weaker. I continued to reassure anyone still listening, perhaps only myself, that the storm would soon be over and played disc after disc of soothing New Age sounds and easy-listening jazz.

My eyelids felt like sandpaper, my tongue was furred from countless cans of Tab. I hadn't eaten since lunch, but couldn't wrap my mind around the simple act of grabbing a piece of chicken from the bucket in the slowly warming refrigerator. It was easier to open another Tab. I was clinging to the edge of sanity, feeling I was hanging by broken fingernails to a ledge that was beginning to crumble. I mindlessly petted Minx and prayed Michael would soon return.

The sky began to lighten at five-thirty. The studio window was so crusted with salt and leaves it was impossible to see clearly. The winds had diminished to intermittent gusts, the rain was once again falling vertically in a steady drizzle.

I picked up Minx, holding her over my shoulder as I left the studio, sloshing my way through the reception area to the inner door, shoving aside the sodden cushions with my foot. The wooden outer door was rain-swollen shut. I pulled the door with such force that when it opened I was knocked on my ass into a puddle.

I grabbed Minx before she could flee, and we went outside into nuclear winter.

Chapter
14

IN EIGHTEEN HOURS St. Chris had been transformed from a verdant tropical paradise into a bleak sepia landscape. Trees completely stripped of their leaves stood broken and skeletal against the silver-gray sky. What little plant life remained was salt dead brown. I had the eerie feeling I was watching *The Wizard of Oz* in reverse, that when I walked through the radio station doorway I'd gone from glowing Technicolor to stark black and white. But there were no cheering Munchkins to welcome me to Oz nor an Auntie Em to comfort me in Kansas. I was on my own in a world familiar yet strange.

The air was still, unbroken by even a warble of birdsong. Mindless of the mud and water, I sank to the step in front of the station and stared, unable to take it all in, at the shattered remains of the buildings around me.

The generator sputtered, then died. WBZE was off the air. I picked myself off the stoop and went to switch the generator over to a full fuel tank. Minx padded behind me, eager for breakfast.

Once we were back on the air, I fed Minx and cleaned out the litter box she'd refused to use—with a disdainful sniff and a haughty glare—after I'd defiled it.

I grabbed the longest-playing classical album I could put my hands on, hit the continuous play button, said God knows what to anyone still listening, put on my bright orange hooded rain poncho, then tacked a scrawled note on the front door that read "at the tower, back soon" and set off on foot to find Michael.

I paused near the Anglican church to look down Kongens Gade toward Fort Frederick. Isabeya's main street was almost impassable. I skirted between sidewalk and roadbed, picking my way around downed tree limbs, blown-away roofing materials, shop signs torn from their frames, and household items I couldn't begin to identify. At the cross streets I waded through torrents of water overflowing the debris-blocked guts, pouring down from the rain-sodden hills to stain the sea dirt brown. The sea had lost its azure sparkle, as if the peacock colors had been sucked into Gilda's eye wall.

It wasn't until I passed Government House and reached the harbor that I saw the full impact of Gilda's fury.

Not one boat was upright. Those left in their harbor moorings had sunk or turned turtle. The boats docked for safety against the boardwalk were now driftwood bobbing in whitecapped waves that crashed against what was left of the boardwalk. I stared openmouthed at the remains of a small cabin cruiser atop the foundation of what had been the small gazebo on the green next to Fort Frederick. When I turned toward the post office I was shocked to see the hull of a good-sized sailboat lying across the narrow street, its stern rail jammed against a signpost that read "Five Minute Parking Only for Postal Patrons."

But it was the sight of Papaya Quay that took my breath away and made me rub my eyes in disbelief.

When Columbus discovered St. Chris in 1493, his fleet

traveled east along our northern coastline until he sighted Papaya Quay. The uninhabited isle was known then by the Indian name Cibuguiera, meaning "stony land," and was used by the Arawak Indians solely as a lookout post.

Gilda had reduced Papaya Quay to its pre-Columbian state.

Harborview looked like a pile of rubble atop a barren knoll stripped of all vegetation. The short dock at the water-sports pavilion was gone; all that remained of the ferry landing were naked pilings, and the ferry itself was nowhere to be seen.

I turned to look at Dockside. The Lower Deck's cobblestone courtyard was now a graveyard for wrecked boats. I watched as a lone figure, shielded from the rain by only a red-and-white-striped Harborview beach towel over its head and shoulders, ran along the gap-toothed boardwalk from the direction of the Watering Hole to disappear near the stone staircase leading to Posh Nosh and Victoria's office. I thought I recognized the spitter, but with the rain and salt spray misting my sunglasses I couldn't be sure.

I pulled my own hood closer to my face and continued walking against the rain along the road toward the WBZE tower. I was halfway there when I heard a police siren. The car stopped just ahead of me and the driver called through the open window, "Curfew is still in effect; return home immediately."

"Benjamin, is that you?"

"Kelly! Why aren't you at the station? What are you doing here?"

I ran to the squad car. "Michael took my car to check the tower during the eye. He never came back."

"Get in. We'll find him."

Benjamin looked as tired and shell-shocked as I felt. I reached over to squeeze his arm. "Are you okay? How did you make out? Where are you headed?"

"Home to check on Camille and Trevor. I haven't heard from them since the phones went out after the eye. What a night."

"Drop me at Soup to Nuts. I can hoof it to the tower from there. You go check on your family."

Benjamin steered the police car over the sidewalk to avoid a pick-up-sticks pile of telephone and power poles tangled in downed lines that blocked most of the street.

"A category five. Who expected it?" I said, shaking my head in disbelief.

"Thank God for life. We're still here," replied Benjamin with a small smile. "Things we can replace. But not people."

He stopped the car at Soup to Nuts, across from the ballpark at the beginning of the east end road. The single-story building was still standing, but the store's galvanized roof curled upward at an angle that reminded me of a Chinese pagoda. I looked over at the ballpark, where the tattered remains of the storefront awning covered third base and a portion of the outfield.

"I'll meet you at the tower, Kelly. Thirty minutes or less. Be careful."

As I approached the tower I saw that it was still upright, but listing at an angle that made the Leaning Tower of Pisa look like a piker. The tower's top section was curled toward the base like a crooked finger.

Where was my car? And where was Michael?

I soon found my car, its roof crushed beneath a downed power pole, the hatch window shattered. I opened the driver side door and saw my new cell phone lying on the passenger seat. The battery was dead. I stuck the phone into my fanny pack and began looking frantically for Michael.

"Michael? Where are you? Come out, come out wherever you are."

I kept calling until I was out of breath.

At last I heard a faint blast from a police whistle.

I took a deep breath and shouted, "Michael, I hear you. Where are you?"

I stood as still as a cat and listened as carefully as Minx would, wishing my ears rotated like hers so I wouldn't have to keep turning my head.

The whistle was repeated. Three short blasts.

Near the base of the tower was a small windowless concrete bunker housing tower equipment.

I wrenched open the door and found Michael lying on the floor.

"Mama, I have a feeling we're not in Kansas anymore."

I knelt to place my hands on either side of Michael's face, tears flowing freely down my own face. I took the whistle and keys from his hand and bent to kiss him gently on the lips, the salt of my tears mingling with his beaded sweat. His face was flushed with fever.

"Benjamin's on the way. We'll get you out of here fast."

"Mama, you were right. I should have stayed at the station. I'm really sorry about your car."

"Things can be replaced. What happened to you?"

"I was calling you from the car when a blast of wind slammed the door on my ankle. Then the pole fell."

"How did you ever get in here?"

Michael managed a faint smile. "Crawled on my belly like a reptile, Mama."

"Let me look at your ankle. I promise I won't touch it."

"You touch, I scream, you die. In that order," Michael said through clenched teeth.

I took one probing look and shuddered, imagining the pain he must be in. "I've seen shapelier ankles on elephants."

"Mama, get me out of here. I'm about to pass out."

I heard a police siren approaching the tower and ran

out to meet Benjamin. "Is everything okay at home?"

"There's a lot of yard work to be done, but Camille and Trevor are fine. They spent most of the storm in our bathroom shower stall with only Trevor's new SnakeLight for illumination. Looks like your car got mashed. Did you find Michael?"

"He's in the bunker with a broken ankle and a bad fever. Can you get him to the hospital?"

"I don't know if we've still got a hospital, but we'll get him there."

After Benjamin and I carried Michael to the police car, I went back to take one last look at the remains of my car. A ten-year-old blue Japanese hatchback with less than forty thousand miles on the odometer. I loved that silly car. There was nothing special about it, except that it got great gas mileage, was easy to park and didn't rust out in the salt air. I put the key in the ignition to see if it still ran. It caught on the first try, but until a crane was available to move that damned pole it wasn't going anywhere. I put the keys in my pocket and quickly cleaned out my glove compartment. I took my tool kit from the hatch, knowing I'd be lucky if the car wasn't stripped for parts by the time I got back to it.

Benjamin dropped me at WBZE before taking Michael to the hospital. "Looks like you're going to be command central for the duration. I'll check back with you later. Tell everyone to stay off the roads while we do a damage assessment."

I leaned into the car to kiss Michael good-bye. "Get well fast, Michael. You know how much I hate hospitals."

Michael's parting shot—"Tell the boss I'm not coming back unless I get a raise"—hung in the air as I opened the front door and went to work.

Chapter
15

WHAT GILDA HADN'T destroyed Sunday evening, the looters took Monday morning.

By midmorning the roads were bumper-to-bumper. Our only national chain store, the so-called Macy's of St. Chris, where we bought everything from twelve-packs of toilet paper to lawn furniture and small appliances, was stripped bare by noon. At the supermarket the remaining shelf stock was just as quickly hauled into waiting cars, freezers emptied of slowly defrosting food. Gun-toting employees stood on the roof at the lumberyard to guard the meager supply of batteries and tarps.

Benjamin arrived at WBZE at one o'clock with two of his deputies.

"Michael's resting comfortably at the hospital—or what's left of it. The airport terminal is gone and the runways are blocked by debris—otherwise we would have tried to get him out. It's a bad break; he won't be able to walk without crutches for several weeks. I need to make an announcement. Will you permit me?"

I set up the mike for Benjamin and cued a tape for later rebroadcasting.

"The entire island of St. Chris is under curfew until further notice. Looting is a serious crime and all looters will be subject to immediate arrest and imprisonment. Anyone caught violating the curfew will be stopped and placed under arrest. Go back to your homes now. The roads are closed to all but emergency vehicles."

We returned to music, and Benjamin wiped his brow.

"Kelly, will you be all right here? Do you have enough food and water? What about fuel for your generator?"

"I stocked up on everything before the storm."

"Is there anyone to relieve you?"

"Everyone's on storm leave. Don't worry about me. I've got Minx; we'll be fine. I'm going off the air at 10 P.M. to get some sleep and give the generator a rest. I'll sign back on tomorrow morning at six."

"Good plan. I'll check in with you later. Keep your doors locked. I fear our islanders are taking out their frustrations against nature on each other." He shook his head. "We should be celebrating life, not stealing from our neighbors. This angers me more than anything I've ever seen."

Minx and I took a KFC break from the bucket in the refrigerator. I moved everything to the freezer, which after several hours without electricity was functioning only as a chill box. I inventoried our food. We'd eat perishables first, saving our canned goods for last. With any luck the bags of ice in the cooler would last for a couple more days. After that, everything we ate or drank would be room temperature.

I had no idea when I'd get home or how I'd get there, or what I'd find when I arrived. I replayed Benjamin's tape and aired a new Dave Grusin jazz album to pass the time.

St. Chris was now as isolated as Pitcairn when the *Bounty* mutineers took up residence. We had no power, no phones, no newspaper, no television, no airport, no immediate links to the outside world.

The skies over St. Chris were clearing, and the winds had died, leaving the air stifling hot and humid. The slowly drying dead leaves in the debris-filled guts were beginning to stink; soon the guts themselves would become breeding grounds for disease-carrying mosquitoes. Jack Spaniard squadrons buzzed in the air, stingers ready to attack, angry that their nests had been destroyed.

I set up my battery-operated shortwave radio in a corner of the studio to try and get a fix on Gilda's current position. I fiddled with the dials, finally pulling in a BBC World Service station broadcasting the late-afternoon Caribbean report.

Static made it difficult to hear, but I gleaned that Gilda had taken a turn to the north bypassing Puerto Rico and the rest of the northern Leewards and was now headed out to sea away from land. I lost my fix on the station and heard no more.

Benjamin stopped by one more time on his way home to get some sleep. "Emergency crews are trying to clear the airport runway. The cruise-ship dock was wrecked by the heavy swells, and the seas are still fierce. I've had reports of people out windsurfing." He smiled wanly. "I'm about to fall asleep on my feet. I hope Camille has some ice left. I'd give anything for a cold drink. I've been living on tepid coffee since yesterday."

"Here's a treat from Michael. He owes you one." I grabbed the last two Heinekens from Michael's six-pack. I'd stashed them in my cooler earlier in the afternoon and was hoarding them for later. We popped the caps from the icy bottles and stood outside the front door, slowly drinking and watching the setting sun falling like a bright copper penny behind the barren west-end hills.

I signed off the air at ten; by ten-fifteen Minx and I were curled together fast asleep on the couch in Mrs. H's office.

Chapter
16

Tuesday morning the National Guard took control of St. Chris and curfew was lifted from 8 A.M. to 6 P.M.

"Our police force is too small to be everywhere; we need help," said Benjamin. "People must be allowed to check on their loved ones, shop owners need to inventory their businesses, my officers still haven't had much sleep. Crews have been working all night working to clear the airport runway. The first military planes coming in from Puerto Rico should be able to land by Friday."

"What's the recovery plan? I haven't heard anything from Government House."

Benjamin chuckled softly. "There's a rumor the governor spent the storm under his bed clutching a bottle of his favorite St. Chris export." The smile left his face. "There's so much to be done, it's difficult to know where to begin. We'll be lucky to have power restored island-wide by Christmas."

Christmas? I remembered saying to Margo we'd be sipping piña coladas on the beach by the weekend. What naive, optimistic fools we'd been.

"The initial assessment shows that ninety percent of the structures on this island were damaged, and many lost their roofs. The entire telephone and electrical system will have to be repaired or replaced. We are running out of fuel, food and water. I fear for the safety of our people unless we get outside help and supplies here soon."

By noon the WBZE reception area had become command central with National Guard and police coming and going, relaying messages and bulletins to be broadcast over the air. I would have given anything for Emily's help at the receptionist desk, but I hadn't seen her since Friday, when she left to go shopping in Puerto Rico over the long holiday weekend.

I looked out of the studio window early in the afternoon to see Maubi's Hot to Trot van pulling into the station parking lot. I ran out to greet him.

"Morning Lady, you making out okay?"

"Maubi, I am so glad to see you."

"How the storm treat you?"

"No complaints. I'm still here. How about you?"

"We make out okay, too. Thank God for life. Can I ask you something?"

"Sure. What is it?"

"Okay if I park here? The guard won't let me pass into town. I got hot food to sell. My wife's home cooking over a coal pot before what we got in the freezer spoils."

"I'll put it on the air—you'll have all the business you can handle."

Word of Maubi's new location spread, and soon the parking lot was jammed with cars. The trash barrel Maubi put out next to his van was overflowing before curfew.

I went out to wish him a good evening and he handed me a paper plate with two beef pates and a chicken leg. Minx stood in the station doorway, her tail quivering.

"I save this for you. Where's Michael? There's a roti waiting for him."

"He's in the hospital with a broken ankle. It's a long story."

"Then he won't be needing this." Maubi handed me a not-quite-cold Heineken. "Good night, Morning Lady. God bless you."

"You too, Maubi. Sleep well. I'll see you in the morning."

Minx and I sat on the stoop in front of the open door, eating our dinner as darkness descended. Without distracting streetlights or house lights, the evening sky was flooded with stars, brighter than I'd ever seen them. I was reminded of nights I'd spent in the Egyptian desert where the stars looked close enough to touch.

Benjamin reappeared at the station Wednesday morning around ten with Rick, one of the weekend part-timers, riding in the passenger seat.

"His family lives close to us. Since there won't be any school for several weeks, he might as well be working. It's time you had a break. I've got a surprise for you. Get in the car."

"Benjamin, did you get any sleep last night? You look exhausted."

"I managed a little nap early this morning. We were out quite late dealing with leads on some of the more avaricious looters." He managed a wan smile. "It appears there will be one less candidate on the Senate ballot this fall."

"What? You don't mean . . ."

"Indeed I do. Mr. Daniel is now residing in the detention center, pending trial. Of course, he tried to claim the fifteen generators he had hidden under blankets in a spare room were destined for the schools. But he had no purchase orders, no receipts, and the merchant said they were part of a shipment that arrived late last week and were still in the warehouse pending customs clearance."

"Why would a man trash his life over a few dollars?"

"Greed and arrogance, Kelly. He thought he was above the law and would never get caught. Our schoolchildren deserve better role models." Benjamin sighed and lapsed into silence.

We drove through town to the WBZE tower. There sat my poor mutilated car, minus its hatch accessory. The downed pole was lying several feet away on the ground.

"I got some of my men out here this morning to free your car. Now you've got wheels again. Let's go check your house."

The east-end countryside looked as devastated as rural Georgia following Sherman's march to the sea. I felt like Scarlett O'Hara heading home after the burning of Atlanta. Had I only been away three days? It seemed like a lifetime. What would I find? Tara or the devastation of Twelve Oaks? I snapped out of my reverie in time to barely avoid sideswiping a downed pole. I took a deep breath and concentrated on my driving.

After a journey that took twice as long as usual because of the debris blocking the road, I turned off the east-end road onto the dirt road that led to my private driveway. When I reached the bottom of the drive I was forced to stop. My driveway was completely washed away; in its place was a gully wider than my car.

I looked up toward my little house, afraid I'd see nothing but ruins. My gallery was finito. Only the concrete slab remained, shorn of screens and roof.

Benjamin and I sidestepped through the bush up to the house, clinging to supple tan-tan branches for support.

The original structure, built of ballast brick and brain coral by the Danes over one hundred years earlier, survived Gilda as it had hurricanes in the past. The interior was dry, but smelled as musty as an old library or seldom-aired attic.

Benjamin and I waded through the tangled brush to open hurricane shutters on the bedroom end of the house to let fresh air flow through to the kitchen. The Jack Spaniards were out in full force and attacked viciously when our hands were too occupied to wave them away.

We sat on the gallery slab drinking tepid water and dabbing Di-Delamine antihistamine gel on our stings. We listened to an atonal symphony of generators, chain saws and drills played to the beat of syncopated hammering, while gazing at bright blue FEMA tarps being installed over roofless houses. Seeing the tarps triggered a childhood memory of mushrooms sprouting after a spring rain.

Benjamin put down his empty water glass. "Kelly, the hospital wants to release Michael this afternoon. They need his bed for really sick people. Some of our old people aren't doing so well."

"Miss Maude?"

"She's fine. She lost most of her fruit trees, but they'll grow back. But Miss Lucinda is in bad shape. She locked herself in a closet for the storm and no one found her until Tuesday afternoon. She was very dehydrated and quite delirious, babbling something about attending a house party with the Prince of Wales. We're all worried about her. I'm worried about Michael, too. He has no place to go when he leaves the hospital."

"What happened to his cottage?"

"The storm took his roof and pitched most of his belongings in the bush. He doesn't know it yet. I'll tell him when Camille and I pass by the hospital."

"He can camp out at the station, or stay here."

"I was hoping you'd say that. The station would probably be best. The doctor wants him off his foot as much as possible for the next two weeks. He'd never make it up your driveway. If you want to come home at night to get away from the station, I can find you a generator for power and light."

"I've got one." I pointed behind me in the direction of

a box in a corner of the living room. "I bought it last week, but haven't used it yet."

"Does it run on propane or regular gas?"

"Both." We walked around to the back of the house, where the two new propane tanks I'd ordered before the storm were still upright.

"Let's get you set up and running."

Soon the generator was hooked up and cooling my refrigerator. I put the food most likely to spoil in the freezer, nestled in the remains of my ice, and hauled out a small gas grill for cooking. Like a fool I'd bought an electric stove when I installed my kitchen. I should have listened to Abby and ordered one that ran on propane. I looked around the rest of my disorderly house and decided that tomorrow was soon enough to think about putting it back in order.

After Benjamin departed, I hauled the plants out of the shower, then stripped out of my filthy clothes and stepped into the shower for the first time in three days. I didn't care that the unheated water was cold enough to raise gooseflesh. My generator wasn't powerful enough to chill the refrigerator and heat water at the same time. I'd rather have a cold Tab than a hot shower. While I washed my hair, I made a mental note of where I'd string a line for drying laundry, realizing my cell-phone money would have been better spent on a more powerful generator.

I sidestepped back down the hill to my car, trying to keep the dirt and grass stains off the clean clothes I'd washed before the storm. Before I went to pick up Michael at the hospital, I needed to check on my friends.

Chapter 17

I STOPPED FIRST at Jerry's and found Jerry, Heidi and Abby sitting on the front gallery drinking lunchtime Bloody Marys. On the back terrace a portable generator roared.

"Got time for your rain check, Kel?"

Why not? Rick was on the air until I returned to relieve him, and I couldn't pick up Michael until two.

"Help yourself, the makings are in the kitchen." Jerry handed me his empty glass. "While you're up, make me one."

I looked around Jerry's house. It didn't look much different than when I'd been there Sunday before the storm. "You got your shutters down fast," I said, handing Jerry his fresh drink.

"I never put them up," he said.

"What? You made it through a category five without your hurricane shutters?"

Heidi looked up from her needlepoint and laughed merrily. "I nagged him all day about putting up those shutters,

Kelly. By the time he got around to it, the rain had already started, so he went to bed after a cold supper and slept through the night. I was the one who was up pacing and listening to the radio. What happened to Michael? I haven't heard him on the air since the storm."

I filled them in on Michael's adventure.

"I like what you've done to your car, Kel," said Abby. "You finally got air-conditioning."

"How did you make out?" I asked.

Abby waggled her hand. "So-so. My house came through all right, but my office is trashed. It's going to take forever to reconstruct my files." She paused to sip her drink. "It's a good thing Margo and Paul got out of here."

"Why?"

"Sea Breezes is a mess. There are roofing tiles all over the parking lot. Port in a Storm was destroyed by the wind and what the wind didn't take, the storm surge washed out to sea. I hear most of the condos have water damage."

"They can stay here when they come back," said Heidi. "We have plenty of room. If you need a place, you're welcome too, Kelly."

"Thanks. I may stop in for R & R when I can get away from the station. My house is in pretty good shape—only the gallery got trashed—but my driveway is gone, and I need a rope tow or a chairlift to get to my front door. I feel like I'm competing in an Eco-Challenge."

Jerry picked up his binoculars and walked to the front of the gallery to stare at the harbor.

"What's happening, Jer?"

"I don't know, but there's a lot of activity out there. Take a look."

I refocused the binoculars. "Where? All I see are boat parts and waves."

"Let me look again."

I turned to say something to Abby, but Jerry interrupted. "Holy shit. They just pulled a body out of the water. Come on, guys—let's get down there and find out what's happening."

We left our drinks on the gallery and abandoned Heidi to sprint down the hill past the post office to the boardwalk, where a small crowd had gathered in front of Dockside.

An inflatable dinghy was slowly trolling back to the area where the Harborview ferry had docked.

Victoria came down the steps from her office with a blanket over her arm.

"Vic!" I ran to hug her. "How did you make out?"

"Kelly! Am I glad to see you! What an absolute trouper you've been. I've been listening to you since Sunday."

"Are you okay?"

"Tip-top. But I've got a hotel full of guests who are anxious to depart. Tempers are wearing quite thin, and my stores of food and water are almost depleted."

"How are your guests going to get off the rock? There aren't any flights."

"The military is bringing in cargo planes with power crews and equipment Friday morning. Seats out are on a first-come, first-served basis."

"Where are the crews going to stay?"

"Here at Dockside. Mine is the only hotel that's habitable. Fortunately, they're bringing their own provisions."

We watched the police divers unload the dinghy. One of the divers removed his hood to shed his face mask for a deep breath of fresh air and promptly threw up into the sea. The noxious stench emanating from the body sent everyone on the narrow boardwalk running back to Dockside. Before a blanket was put into service as a shroud, I glanced at the body and gasped when I saw the battered, bloated face of the homeless woman known as the spitter. Then, like the diver, I tossed my cookies into the sea.

Chapter
18

MICHAEL WAS NOT his usual laid-back self.

When I picked him up at the hospital his first complaint was about my thirty-minute tardiness. Before I could tell him about the body, he demanded I drive him to the west end to inspect the remains of his rented cottage.

As Benjamin reported earlier, Michael's roof had indeed gone bush, along with most of his possessions. However, his cherished Harley was still where he'd left it Sunday afternoon, safely parked in Mrs. H's office.

"Leave me here, Mama. I want to deal with this mess."

"Michael, are you demented? You've got a broken ankle. How are you going to do anything? You can barely walk. The doctor wants you off that foot. Come with me to the station and sack out in Mrs. H's office. I've got to relieve Rick so he can get home before curfew."

"I'm not going anywhere tonight. Come back for me tomorrow." He hobbled into his cottage and slammed the front door. The impact sent ripples fluttering through his new blue tarp roof.

"Have it your way," I yelled, "but I think you're behaving like a bratface." I jumped in my car and fumed all the way back to the station.

Maubi had already departed for the day when I got back to the station a few minutes after four. Benjamin stopped by to pick up Rick at four-thirty. "Where's Michael?"

"At home."

"How did he ever make it up your hill?"

"Not my house. His."

Benjamin gave me a knowing look and told Rick to wait in the car. "Some people are really stressed out by the storm. I'll pass by and check on him tomorrow." He handed me an emergency pass. "You look like you need a rest. I suggest you spend tonight in the quiet of your own home. This will get you past the curfew roadblocks. I'm going home for dinner with Camille and Trevor and a good rest myself, after a quick trip to the hospital morgue. Did you hear about the body in the harbor?"

"I was there when the divers brought her ashore."

"As I might have guessed." He shook his head sadly. "An unfortunate person, our only human casualty of the storm. She carried no identification, so we don't know for sure who she was. She should have passed the storm in the shelter at the Anglican church."

"I know who she was. The spitter."

"The what?" said Benjamin.

"That's what they called her at the Watering Hole. I never knew her real name."

"Now I remember. We had some complaints about her."

"How did she die?"

"Apparently a drowning. She must have slipped on the boardwalk or been caught by the surge during the storm. She's been dead for several days."

"I don't think the storm killed her," I said. "I saw her on the boardwalk Monday morning when I was heading for the tower to look for Michael. I'll bet you a hot meal and a cold drink there was foul play involved."

Benjamin held out his hand. "I'll take that bet. We will talk more about this in the morning. What time do you want Rick here for work?"

"Until I've got more staff, he's on a ten-to-four shift. I'll sign on at six, then relieve him in the afternoon and sign off at ten."

"For those hours he can manage transportation on his bicycle."

At 10 P.M. I signed off for the evening. After tucking a sleepy Minx inside her carrier, we headed home along the deserted roads to sleep in our very own beds for the first time since the storm.

Chapter
19

IN SPITE OF the generator rumbling through the night, sounding like a freight train passing outside my kitchen door, I slept soundly until my battery-operated alarm clock went off at four-thirty Thursday morning.

I showered once again in unheated water, then emptied and refilled all my ice trays before popping the top on a frosty-cold Tab. The bubbly liquid slithering down my throat tasted better than Jerry's Easter Sunday morning Perrier-Jöuet.

Minx, having circumnavigated the kitchen looking for her food and water dishes, returned to her starting point to swipe my bare ankle with her paw—a gesture that immediately got my undivided attention. She sat looking at me through lemonade eyes narrowed to slits the size of slivers from the true cross, and I realized I'd forgotten to bring home her favorite dishes and paw-print mat from Mrs. H's office. An oversight not destined to win the heart of a hungry feline who had watched too many Fancy Feast commercials and knew she deserved only the best, properly served.

To make amends, I grabbed a single-serving tin of special-treat Sheba from the cupboard and emptied it onto a small paper plate.

"Chow down, tiny tiger. I'll bring your regular dishes home with me tonight."

Food won out over presentation. I filled a plastic quart ice-cream container with water and set it on the floor. I salivated at the thought of ice cream for breakfast—a traditional Christmas morning treat that Minx and I both relished—and wondered if the St. Chris dairy would be open and making rum raisin ice cream again by Christmas.

Except for my wristwatch and the battery-operated clock ticking next to my bed, every time-keeping device in my house was going blinky-blinky-blinky like a cheap set of multihued Christmas twinkie lights. The strobe effect, coupled with the noise of the generator, was giving me a headache. I unplugged everything that blinked, grabbed a flashlight and a fresh Tab and went outside to turn off the generator. Benjamin had warned me not to run it more than six hours at a time, and to store it inside the house when I wasn't using it. "Generators are in very short supply, and you don't want that one tiefed." He also advised me to keep the boards over my sliding glass doors until my gallery was rebuilt; and to bolt my hurricane shutters when I was away from the house.

Minx came outside for her postbreakfast bath and joined me on the gallery slab. I fiddled with the tuning band of my small shortwave radio trying to locate the BBC World Service and found instead a station from San Juan broadcasting in English.

"And now for the Caribbean weather. A slow-moving, weak tropical wave is approaching the northern Leewards, expected to pass over St. Chris tonight and reach the San Juan metroplex late Friday afternoon. There are no winds associated with this system; however, rainfall will measure two to four inches and residents in low-lying areas should be aware of potential flood conditions."

I ran inside to scribble some notes and listen to the rest of the news broadcast. Programming at WBZE had been free-form since the storm, mostly local announcements with brief musical interludes while the deejays made pit stops, but I wanted to get back to a more standardized format.

When I went back outside to haul in the generator, Minx had disappeared on safari. She'd been so good about being confined in the station, spending most of her time sequestered in Mrs. H's office, that I made no effort to look for her. We both needed some quiet time by our-selves.

The roads back to Isabeya were still traffic-free because of curfew. I signed on promptly at six and began the day with a newscast culled from what I'd heard on the San Juan station, ending with the weather forecast. I empha-sized that the approaching system was only a tropical wave, but reminded listeners who had not yet secured tarps for their roofs that considerable rainfall was antici-pated.

Jerry was my first visitor, bearing a paper plate filled with Heidi's famous homemade cinnamon rolls. They were still warm from the oven, and icing was dripping down the sides of each roll and onto the plate. I snagged some frosting and licked it off my finger.

"We have a gas stove," he said, helping himself. "Got any coffee?"

"I can manage a cup of instant."

Jerry made an ugly face. "No, thanks. What else have you got?" He settled for a bottle of fruit punch from Em-ily's shelf in the refrigerator.

"Heidi kicked me out of the house. She said I'm driving her nuts. Kel, I don't know what to do with myself. I can't play golf, the Watering Hole is still closed because there's no power and obviously there's no real estate business."

"Go down to Government House at eight, ask for Chris and tell him I sent you. They're looking for someone who knows the island to work on the disaster relief program, and you'd be perfect. It's walking distance from your house and it's a paid position. You'll be right in the center of everything that's happening."

Jerry threw his arms around me in a big hug. "Thanks, Kel. Keep the rest of the rolls." He stopped in the studio doorway. "There was another reason I came by. We're having a potluck party Saturday afternoon at our place. It's BYO food and booze, and ice if you've got any, but we'll supply the place and cooking facilities. Hope you can make it."

"I'll be there if I have to shut down the station."

"Bring Michael if he's out of the hospital."

"I'll tell him about it."

Benjamin was my next gentleman caller. "Where did you get those rolls? Don't tell me you got up early to bake?"

"On a gas grill? I don't think so. Please help yourself. I haven't got any coffee, but I can offer you a bottle of juice."

His mouth was too full of cinnamon roll to respond verbally, but he nodded his acceptance of the juice offer. I handed him a tissue to wipe the frosting from his chin.

"I'm the one who owes you a hot meal and a cold drink. You were right. There was foul play involved in the spitter's death. The base of her skull was smashed. She was dead before she hit the water."

Chapter
20

I HAD TWO stops I wanted to make in the six hours I had
free after Rick arrived for his shift.

First, I went to visit Miss Maude, bringing her the last
of the cinnamon rolls.

"Kelly, I am so glad to see you. I've been wondering
about you. Come. Sit on the gallery, and I'll bring us
some hot tea."

I'd never been inside Miss Maude's stone house, built
by her father around the time of the transfer from Denmark, and didn't feel it was polite to enter unless invited.
I sat in the chair she indicated and looked at her side yard,
where vegetable and herb gardens were laid out in tidy
rows next to the fruit-tree orchard. Most of the trees had
been pruned to bare limbs or stumps. The downed limbs
were reduced to piles of logs stacked next to a domed
brick structure.

Miss Maude reappeared with a teak tray loaded with
her mother's china tea service and delicate porcelain cups
with matching saucers. "If you don't mind, I'll take those

lovely rolls to Lucy when I visit her after lunch. You know how she adores her sweets."

"How is Miss Lucinda?"

"Better than she lets on," said Miss Maude with a smile. "I was quite worried when I found her in the linen closet—she'd been through a very trying ordeal, the poor dear didn't realize she had the closet-door key tucked in her pocket—but I think now she's enjoying all the attention."

"Did you make out all right? It looks like your fruit trees took quite a beating."

"They'll survive, and so will I," said Miss Maude, handing me a cup of Earl Grey tea. "Hurricanes are nature's cleanser. You'll see. Everything will come back stronger and better than before. And what's destroyed perhaps wasn't meant to be. I remember the hurricane of 1928. Lucy had been here only a few months as a new bride. I know she appears now to be a silly, sometimes foolish, woman, but she has quite a good head on her shoulders. After that storm, which completely destroyed our small hospital, she turned her own home into a makeshift hospital and later led the fund-raising campaign to build the one we still use today. Times were different then. We helped each other more and also relied more upon our neighbors. St. Chris was a true community."

"I had no idea Miss Lucinda was such a dynamo. Please give her my best when you see her."

"Indeed I shall. And you? How did you fare? I see what the storm did to your car. How about your house? And your sweet Minx? Is she all right?"

"Minx is fine. I'm not sure I would have gotten through the storm without her. Especially after the eye, when I was so worried about Michael."

Miss Maude poured me another cup of tea. "Benjamin told me of Michael's adventure. How is he doing now?"

I sighed. "I'm not sure. His ankle seems to be healing, but I think he's lost his sense of humor."

"Some people need time to find their strength. You're one of the strong ones, Kelly; you will never lose that. Michael will come around. If he doesn't, perhaps this island isn't where he needs to be. There isn't anything you can do to change that. All you can do is leave him alone until he finds himself."

I mulled over what Miss Maude had said while listening to the frenzied chirping of tiny black-winged, yellow-bellied sugar birds clustered around the coconut-shell feeder hanging on the end of her gallery.

"Those are the first birds I've seen since the storm," I said.

"The birds will survive. Better than some humans," she replied with a smile. "But they sometimes need a little help. I'll give you an extra feeder to take home with you. Put it someplace Minx can't get to it and keep it filled with cornmeal mixed with sugar."

"It's so quiet and peaceful out here." I realized why when I looked around and didn't see a generator. "Miss Maude, where do you keep your generator?"

She laughed before replying. "Kelly, this house was built long before electricity was available on St. Chris. I didn't need a generator then, and I don't need one now. Come inside, and I'll show you why."

She led me through the double-door entrance into a spacious living room filled with antique furniture, carefully positioned on muted hand-woven carpets atop the polished wide-plank floors. Bookcases on short sides of the rectangular room, overflowing with leather-bound volumes, served as room dividers separating the living room from the bedrooms on the west end, and from the kitchen and dining room on the east. On the far wall was a second set of double doors opening onto the back gallery running the full length of the house.

"Miss Maude, your home is like a museum. It's absolutely beautiful."

"This is the house I've lived in since 1917. Those chairs were Mama's and Papa's, where they would sit every night after dinner while Papa read to us by lanternlight. The desk was his, too. I was married here in the back garden in 1927. Out there"—she pointed to the west—"is our family burial plot."

Miss Maude took me into her kitchen. "This is what I wanted to show you." She pointed to an old-fashioned hand pump built into the counter next to her deep double-wide sink. "When you have the repair work done on your house, I suggest you have an outside pump installed. That way you'll never be without water. Even though I have a gas stove and refrigerator, I still occasionally use the brick oven Papa built out back. I have kerosene lamps for light, as we did when the house was built. I begged Papa for gaslights, like the ones in the ballroom at Government House, but he said they were far too extravagant." Her blue eyes began to twinkle. "However, Papa was the one who convinced the former colonial council to have electricity installed throughout the island. It's certainly made life easier, but I think we've lost our self-reliance. We've become too dependent on complicated machinery we don't know how to fix that we've forgotten how to fend for ourselves."

We headed back to the living room. "Wait here for a minute; I brought you a little present from Denmark. I'll go get it." She disappeared down the passage leading to the bedrooms.

I wandered over to the desk, worth more on the antique market than the entire contents of my house including my jewelry. The rolltop was open to expose neatly organized pigeonholes. On the desktop lay a hard-bound book with a bright blue cover. The title of the book was in Danish.

Miss Maude came back holding a small paper-wrapped parcel. "I've been doing some family research. The book you're looking at is Krak's *Blaa Bog,* the Danish social register."

"Really? How interesting. Could you look up someone for me?"

"Certainly. What is the name?"

"Christian Thorsen."

Miss Maude quickly thumbed through the pages. "There's no Thorsen listed. Are you sure you have the correct spelling?"

"I think so; I'll double-check."

"Why are you so interested? I didn't know you knew anyone in Denmark."

"I don't. And I doubt if the person who gave me that name does either."

"Are you on the track of another mystery? If I can be of any assistance, please let me know." Miss Maude smiled. "Now, open your present. I will say that when I bought it, I had no idea we would be affected by the events of last weekend."

I eagerly opened the parcel. Inside was a book titled *1867: Disaster in the Danish West Indies.*

"This is a new English translation of a Danish work long out of print. I have a copy of the Danish original from Papa's library, and thought you would enjoy this as you are interested in St. Chris history."

"I'm deeply touched. Thank you for thinking of me."

"You'll find the book is inscribed. The translator is an old and very dear friend of mine."

On the flyleaf was a personal inscription. "That makes this book even more special. Thank you. I'll start reading it tonight. By the way, what happened in 1867?"

"That was the year that hurricanes, earthquakes and tidal waves almost destroyed St. Chris. There is always much we can learn from our history."

Chapter
21

CHECKING ON MICHAEL was the second stop on my list, but after my chat with Miss Maude I decided to let him be.

I still had four hours until I needed to be back at the station. It was time to treat myself to some R & R. First I cleared the path to the cove where I usually moored Top Banana, then went home, turned on the generator to keep the refrigerator going, and put on my oldest swimsuit and a pair of ratty tennis shoes.

I carefully maneuvered Top Banana down the gully to where my car was parked. When I tried to raise the hatch, I realized I'd made a huge mistake. The frame was so badly dented I couldn't open the hatch with a crowbar. I could haul my kayak back up the hill to the house, carry it a quarter mile to the cove or lash it to the top of my car where it fit snugly in the pole dent. Back to the house for some rope, and half an hour later I was shoving off into the Caribbean Sea.

In the four days since the storm, the ocean swells had

subsided to sun-dappled wavelets, but the water was still murky. I missed being able to look through clear azure water to watch small blue-and-yellow fish playing hide-and-seek in the coral.

I paddled out to the reef where the iron rod that marked the uncharted entrance was still erect, though the orange Day-Glo ribbon that was always tied to it had been blown to bits by Gilda. After tying on to the rod, I slid out of Top Banana into the bathwater-warm ocean—water much warmer than the rainwater stored in my cistern.

I lay in the ocean, floating on my back with my eyes closed, drifting slowly with the westward-flowing current. I felt the tensions of the past week beginning to dissipate. I turned briefly on my stomach in a dead man's float, and wondered what it felt like to drown—and hoped I would never find out. I remembered the spitter hadn't died from drowning, she'd died from a battered skull. That was something I didn't want to experience firsthand either. I didn't really know the woman, but hoped her death had been swift. I couldn't imagine why anyone would want to kill a homeless person.

I raised my arm to check the time on my waterproof watch. Ninety minutes to go before work. I glanced to the east to check the position of my kayak, and realized I'd made another blunder. Getting back to Top Banana was going to take a hell of a swim against the current, and the easterly skies were beginning to fill with dark storm clouds.

Minx was waiting at the kitchen door when I sprinted up the hill carrying my kayak paddle. The first raindrops were falling as I dragged the still-hot generator inside. My first priority would be to build some sort of waterproof protective housing. I had a lot to learn about living without conventional electric power. Miss Maude was right about sacrificing self-reliance for convenience. I felt like a city slicker.

I fed Minx and quickly dressed for work, donning my hooded orange rain poncho for the downhill trek to my car. I grabbed some plastic trash bags to stuff around the hatch frame to keep the rain from turning my car into a swamp. It already smelled musty from exposure to Gilda.

Maubi was gone when I arrived at the WBZE parking lot. In the space he'd occupied earlier was a familiar bronze BMW. I ran inside and found Margo sitting in the reception area. She jumped up and threw her arms around me.

"Look what the storm blew in. God, am I glad to see you."

"Oh, Kel, I can't believe what happened to our beautiful island."

"When did you get back? I thought the St. Chris airport was still closed."

"The runway is ninety-five percent cleared. We landed an hour ago. Paul wanted to get home before the military planes starting coming in tomorrow. We spent last night in San Juan in that god-awful airport hotel."

"You mean El Fleabag Tacky Grande Hotel Whorehouse and Rescue Mission? I've had to stay there a couple of times myself when a cheap airline was picking up the room tab after getting me into San Juan too late to make my connection to St. Chris. The only thing going for that place is that it beats spending the night locked in a stall in the ladies' room."

"St. Chris is going to be a real zoo, Kel. The carpetbaggers are coming in droves. There are mobs of people trying to get over here from San Juan. Power crews, insurance adjusters, contractors, there are even some media reps still hanging around waiting to get a look at this place."

"Tell me how you made out. I haven't been over to Sea Breezes, but Abby said it was hit hard."

"It looks worse than it actually is. Our unit came through pretty well. But we're staying at Jerry's for a couple of nights until we figure out how to deal with power and water. Can you join us for dinner? Let's have a drink and sit and talk. I really missed you. I want to hear about everything."

"Sweetie, I'd love to, but I can't tonight. I'm on the air from four until ten and back here again at six tomorrow morning. Let's get together during the day tomorrow. I'm off from ten until four."

"Where's Michael? Haven't you got any help?"

"It's a long story, Margo. We'll talk tomorrow, I promise. Why don't I meet you at Sea Breezes about ten-thirty and we'll see about getting your condo in shape."

"Works for me. Oh, Kel, I forgot to tell you. Guess who I ran into in the St. Chris airport this afternoon? Leila Mae. I guess she's finally had enough of this place. She offered Paul a thousand dollars to fly her to San Juan immediately."

"What did he say?"

Margo smiled. "You're going to love this. He told her to take a hike."

Chapter
22

I CURLED UP with Minx on my big brass bed, listening to the rain pound on my galvanized tin roof. Rain is always a blessing on an island without a fresh-water supply. After a good rain I sometimes celebrate by indulging in two hot showers a day.

This tropical wave was good news/bad news. Good news about the water gushing through the reconnected downspouts to fill my cistern, bad news that there were more cold showers in my immediate future. What I really needed was a solar water heater. How soon could I get one by mail order? In my head I heard Miss Maude chuckling. I aimed my flashlight on the bedside notepad where I scribbled: (1.) build generator housing, (2.) make solar-heated shower. Miss Maude nodded her approval.

The trouble was I couldn't run to the nearest hardware store for parts. Since the storm, we hadn't seen one plane or ship. Food supplies were down to what people had on hand in their cupboards and ice cubes were more precious than gold ingots, and as I lay in my snug bed, listening to the rain on my roof, I couldn't help but wonder and worry about those who had lost their roofs and hoped they were keeping dry this rainy night. Suddenly my wish for hot water seemed very petty indeed.

I glanced at my battery-operated clock. Almost midnight, and I had to be up again in less than five hours. These double-shift days were becoming a real drag. If some of my regular staff, including Michael, didn't get their asses back to work PDQ, I'd be looking for new help. Being the boss was the pits. When any of the regular deejays didn't show, it was either me or dead air.

I burrowed under the sheet out of striking range of the ravenous mosquito hoards, whose high-pitched screeching made me want to stuff cotton in my ears and wish for an army of rapier-tongued lizards to flick those little kamikazes from the air. I opened the book Miss Maude brought me from Denmark to read the first chapter before turning off my flashlight.

I was immediately transported back to the St. Chris of 1867.

Isabeya, no longer a favored port on the molasses sector of the triangular trade route after the importation of slaves was banned by the Danes in 1803, had become a hub of Caribbean commerce. Down-island schooners sailed in and out of the harbor from neighboring British, French and Dutch islands, and ships from Europe flying flags of England, Spain, Denmark and France were often in port. Pirate ships were known to travel the Caribbean waters.

The Customs House (now our local library) and neighboring Scale House, where goods were weighed and taxed (presently home to the Department of Tourism), were the center of daily activity. Along the wharf were storehouses built of native stone, crammed with goods.

The planters dominated the countryside with sugar and cotton plantations, but in Isabeya, the merchants ruled.

When Isabeya was rebuilt after the devastating fire of

1764, sugarcane was the main cash crop. The wealthier planters built homes in town (the same structures that now house our tourist shops, offices and banks) filled with handsome furniture created from the hardwood forests they destroyed to clear land for planting sugarcane. The merchants lived in town year-round in spacious residences built over their ground-floor shops.

The increasing production of beet sugar sent cane prices into a decline that began in 1820. The glory days of sugar were over in St. Chris, although sugar would remain a major crop for another one hundred years.

Denmark was already in negotiations with the United States for the sale of St. Chris for five million dollars in gold. Under the terms of the 1733 agreement, when France sold St. Chris to Denmark, the Danes could not sell to anyone without France's approval. Napoleon III strongly disapproved of the proposed sale; but the United States, under the direction of Secretary of State William Henry Seward, continued to pursue discussions with Denmark. In fall of 1867—when hurricanes were no longer an ongoing threat to safe sea passage—a delegation was sent to St. Chris to meet with Danish officials. Denmark needed the money, and the United States desired a military base in the Caribbean. A deal was in the making.

I marked my place, closed the book and turned off my flashlight. With Minx's spine pressed against my side like Velcro, her slow rhythmic breathing matching my own, we fell asleep to the sound of rushing water.

Chapter
23

I woke early Friday morning, before the alarm jolted me into an instantly crabby mood, to the continuing sound of rain.

Sidestepping down the muddy slope that masqueraded as my driveway reminded me of the greasy pole contest at our annual Agricultural Fair. I looked at my dirt-spattered feet and legs and was again grateful not to be in a dress-for-success occupation. There are advantages to radio. As long as I don't trip over my tongue, no one cares what I look like—least of all me.

At four-thirty I turned onto the east-end road toward Isabeya. I flitted through town, waving my emergency pass at the National Guard officers patrolling the main roads, and reached Michael's house a few minutes after five.

It was still too dark to see clearly, but I heard the rain plop, plop, plop on his blue-tarp roof, then gurgle through the aluminum downspouts to his cistern. His window shutters were tightly closed, and there was no response to my repeated knocking. I hesitated, not wanting to be mistaken for a prowler or set off any battery-operated alarms, then gently turned the knob on his front door. The door was securely locked. The house felt deserted. Where had he gone?

I ran to my car to scribble a brief note that I tucked in his doorframe, then headed to the station to perform generator maintenance before I signed on at six. We were running low on fuel. One of my afternoon chores would be stopping at the fuel depot to beg for a delivery. I didn't stand a prayer of getting more propane delivered to my house—only a sure-footed goat or a deer descended from the original herd brought by the Knights of Malta could navigate that slippery slope. A couple more weeks of hauling, and I'd qualify for Sherpa status on Everest. I glanced in the backseat of my car to make sure I'd remembered the gas containers I needed for home generator use.

I darted through the rain to the front door of the station. Before I could put my key in the lock, the door swung slowly inward. My heart began to pound, and I thought I'd become an instant candidate for Depends.

I remembered a brief sidebar in the last issue of the *Coconut Telegraph* published the day of the storm, denying a rumor that the inmates in our local prison—former Danish barracks less than a half mile from the station—were to be released before the storm hit. Two of those inmates had been after me before and would welcome the slightest excuse to make my life miserable again.

Perhaps I've read too many mystery novels. There was no way I was going into that dark deserted radio station by myself like one of those brainless twits who ends up in deep doo-doo. Color me as yellow as Top Banana, but fem-jep isn't really my thing.

I quickly pulled the door shut and locked the dead

bolt—as I remembered having done less than eight hours earlier—then sprinted to my car. I headed back to the barricade at the nearby Anglican church, where I'd last seen the National Guard.

Five minutes later, accompanied by two armed guard officers, I returned to the station.

I unlocked the door and stood back on the stoop to allow the officers to precede me. I held my flashlight overhead, feeling like the Statue of Liberty, to illuminate the entranceway as they entered with their own lights and drawn guns. I stayed in the doorway as they proceeded through the reception area toward the studio and offices.

From the back of the station I heard one of the officers call out, "Hands up or I'll shoot."

A familiar voice replied, "I work here, man; what's going on?"

I headed for Mrs. H's office to find Michael, clad only in leopard-print briefs and leg cast, standing at attention with his arms raised over his head, facing the officers whose guns were aimed at his more vulnerable body parts. It was definitely a Kodak moment.

Whether it was from relief or the absurdity of the situation, I laughed until tears dripped off my chin and my stomach hurt. "It's okay," I said, when I finally recovered my voice, "this man *does* work here. I'm sorry to have bothered you."

The officers departed with my heartfelt thanks and the promise of a free hot lunch and cold drink at Maubi's Hot to Trot when they were off duty, and I went back into the office to deal with Michael.

"You scared the piss out of me, Michael. What in the hell did you think you were doing? I stopped at your house this morning, and you weren't there."

Michael reached out to put his arms around me.

"Uh-uh. Not until you've brushed your teeth. You've got bat breath. I'll tend to the generator and meet you in the studio. If you're really good, I'll let you brew one pot of coffee, but no a/c and no lights. We're running low on fuel."

After my usual sign-on, I segued into the soundtrack album from *Doctor Zhivago*. No one needed reminding how hot it was and how hot it was going to remain for months to come as we struggled to live without electrical power for fans and air-conditioning.

Rick and I had decorated the studio walls with pictures of cold things—frosty drinks, trips to the mountains, even ads for refrigerator/freezer combos—torn from the magazines in the reception area, the illusion of cold being almost as good as cold itself. I'd scoured the music library for any albums relating to chillier temps—Edvard Grieg's *Peer Gynt Suite* would be featured next on the morning classics.

We'd also instituted the great "how many ways can you fix canned tuna?" contest, soliciting recipes from St. Chris residents to be dropped off at the station and read over the air. I decided to publish the daily winners in a booklet to be printed and distributed as the WBZE Christmas giveaway. When and if my advertising sales staff returned to work, I'd send them out to all our advertisers to offer a free print ad in the booklet with every new advertising contract for airtime.

Michael hobbled into the studio, his hands occupied with coffee mug and cane, looking more like his usual self in a pair of baggy shorts and a luridly flowered Hawaiian shirt.

"I liked the briefs," I said, making no attempt to hide the smile on my face.

"You should, Mama; you gave them to me."

"Michael, how did you get to the station? There's a curfew on. I know you weren't here when I left at ten-thirty."

"Ben brought me. He stopped at my place on his way

home last night. We talked for a couple of hours. He made me realize what a self-centered jerk I've been."

I said nothing, but kept an eye on the remaining time left on the album as "Lara's Theme" went out over the airwaves.

"He also pointed out that you'd been shouldering the whole load here this week with only Rick for backup."

"Rick's done a great job. I'll be sorry to lose him when he graduates from high school next year. I think he's got a real future in broadcasting, and I'm going to write a college recommendation for him. He could be scholarship material."

"Mama, I'm back if you want me, and I'll work any hours you set up. But if you fire me, I understand. I'm sorry I let you down. You deserve better."

I thought for a minute before replying. "Michael, you remember when you first asked me out? I said no because I didn't want to mix business with personal. I still don't, I don't think it's professional, but it's a little late for that. So, let's deal with this one area at a time. First, your job."

Michael's eyes remained fixed on mine.

"When you went to the tower during the eye, it was against my better judgment. It was a stupid thing to do. And I'm not talking about my car."

"I'll buy you a new one."

"That's not the point. As I said before, things can be replaced but not people. I need you here, Michael; the station needs you. No one else does the night shift like you. I want you on the air. I'll set up the schedule today."

"We can go back to 24/7 beginning tonight."

"Not while there's a curfew and we're still on generator power. We'll continue to sign off at ten. I've got to go out this afternoon to beg for fuel and more parts. We can't run the generator twenty-four hours a day. It'll crash, and we'll be off the air permanently."

Michael nodded.

"Now for the personal. Because I'm putting you on the four-to-ten shift, I think it's best if you hole up here until you're able to ride your bike again. My driveway's gone, so there's no way you can make it up to my house."

"Are you saying I've blown it? That we're through?"

"No, I'm not saying that at all. I'm tired, every day is a new set of problems and it's not even been a week since the storm. I have to put the station first. It's my job to keep this place running."

"Where does that leave us?"

"I don't know. This is my home, Michael. I'm here for the duration. You need to decide if this is really where you want to be."

"Fair enough. Ben and I talked about it last night. He said . . ."

I placed my index finger across his lips. "Let's not talk about it now. Let's just get through each day as it comes. I can take you home later if you want to pick up some of your stuff. There's a BYO party tomorrow afternoon at Jerry's if you want to go with me."

Michael got up to refill his coffee cup. Before he left, he put his arms around me. His kiss was like a cool mountain breeze.

Chapter
24

I BEAT MARGO to Sea Breezes. The condo complex didn't look nearly as bad as Abby had described it. Unglazed Mexican roofing tiles were heaped on the far side of the curving driveway. Some of the parked cars looked like they'd been hit by a meteor shower, but all appeared mobile.

The tropical wave was slowly moving westward toward Puerto Rico. Skies over St. Chris were beginning to lighten from gunmetal to pewter, and the rain was more sprinkles than showers. I left my rain poncho in my car and walked toward the beach, following a trail of meat-scented smoke, grateful to feel air on my skin rather than heat-sealing plastic.

Mitch called to me from inside Port in a Storm.

"Hey, Kelly, want some breakfast? The selection's limited, but it's hot."

"Mitch, this place looks great. I heard everything was washed out to sea."

"Don't believe rumors. We lost a couple of sliding glass

doors, and the furniture was rearranged, but we're in good shape. I've got a gas stove, and a generator hooked up to the refrigerator and icemaker. We're having nightly cook-outs on the beach because all the condos have electric stoves. I've got more business here than I can handle. I won't reopen to the public until I get more food and a generator big enough to handle the walk-in freezer, but you're welcome anytime. You got something you want cooked, bring it over. How about a Bloody on the house?"

I smiled when I saw a hand-lettered sign over the bar that read, "Limit two ice cubes per drink. NO exceptions."

Margo found me having a Bloody with Mitch. "Oh, I want one of those. Put it on my tab. I just came from a war zone."

Mitch and I quickly responded with:

"Where?"

"What's going on?"

"The airport. Sorry I'm late, Kel. I didn't think I was going to get out of there alive." She paused for a healthy swig of her drink. "People are killing each other to get out of here. Tourists are running around with fistfuls of cash trying to get a seat on anything with wings, kids are screaming and hitting each other. The guard has formed a barricade around what's left of the terminal. It's ugly. I'm damned glad to be home."

"I haven't seen anything flying this morning," said Mitch.

"It's nasty between here and San Juan. This tropical wave really screwed up the flight schedule. Paul's grounded until the weather clears. Guess who I saw throwing his weight around trying to get a free ride?"

I took one of the ice-cube slivers from my mouth and slid it back into my drink. "Who?"

"Your nemesis from the parade committee. Mr. Daniel."

"Wait a minute—he's in jail."

"What? Fill me in."

"He was arrested for looting."

Margo's cat-that-ate-the-canary smile said it all.

"I'd give anything for a phone. I need to get in touch with Benjamin. Mitch, thanks for the drink. Margo, I'll catch you later, okay?"

"Come back for the barbeque tonight. Damn, that's right—you've got to work."

"I've got help. I can be here."

"What about curfew?"

"I've got a pass. Sweetie, I've got to run. I'll be back in a bit."

I met Benjamin in the police-station parking lot. "This is none of my business, but I heard that Mr. Daniel is at the airport trying to hitch a ride off the rock."

Benjamin looked grim. "Thanks for the tip. We'll see about Mr. Daniel's travel plans. No one's going anywhere for a few hours. If you're smart, you'll stay as far away from the airport as you can get. Do me a favor and put it on the air. Tell everyone to stay away unless they've got official business to transact. I don't want to be responsible if someone gets hurt."

"I'm on my way. It'll be on the air in a few minutes. And Benjamin?"

He paused at the door of his patrol car.

"Thanks for talking to Michael."

"Give him some time, Kelly; he'll be okay. Things might work out even better than you think. I talked to him like a Dutch uncle."

We pulled out of the parking lot, heading in opposite directions.

I went back to WBZE to give Rick the on-air announcement and his new hours. I'd fill my regular six-to-noon slot, Rick would be on from noon to four, and Michael would do the four-to-ten shift. But until we had more help, there were no days off for anyone.

"Where's Michael? I offered him a lift home."

"He was out talking to Maubi. Then Miss Maude came by to see you. I think he hitched a ride with her."

I ran out to pay Maubi for two lunches and drinks for the guard officers.

"How are you holding up, Maubi?"

"Hanging in with the strong ones, Morning Lady. You doing okay?"

"I'm good, but we're running out of fuel."

"Me too. After today I'll be cooking here on a coal pot, same as home. They too busy at the fuel place to deal with me."

"I'm on my way there now."

I stood in line in the heat and humidity for over an hour before getting to the front door. The queue was orderly, no pushing or shoving. We all had storm stories to relate. I saw strangers hugging and saying "Thank God for life." One woman stood quietly with two small children at her side, reading her Bible.

A sign on the depot door read: "CASH ONLY. No checks, no credit. No exceptions."

I was buzzed inside to plead my case.

"Kelly, we'd like to help you out. You get us cash by four and we'll fill your propane tanks before curfew. Everyone needs fuel, and we're not taking a chance on getting stiffed with bad checks. Who knows when the banks will reopen?"

Damn. We had no cash at WBZE. I'd made a deposit a week earlier before the banks closed for the storm. Our petty cash consisted of loose change and postage stamps. I quickly drove home to clean out every last dollar from the emergency stash in my floor safe. I was left with some foreign currency hidden in a double-decker bus toffee tin I'd bought at Heathrow, and a few low-denomination traveler's checks from my last vacation in Egypt.

Minx rubbed her face against my bare leg while I sat

cross-legged on my closet floor counting my cash. I picked her up, holding her at eye level, and we rubbed foreheads. It made me feel better. I filled her food and water dishes before heading back down the hill.

After paying for the fuel, I had less than twenty dollars cash to my name. I went back to WBZE to await the delivery that would get us through another week.

Maubi was emptying his trash barrel.

"Don't go anywhere," I said. "The cavalry is on the way with fuel."

Maubi blinked rapidly and turned to reach for a paper napkin. I saw him duck his head to wipe his eyes. I put my hand on his shoulder. "Friends help friends. I wouldn't be here if it weren't for your son Quincy. I haven't forgotten what he did for me last spring."

"Let's have a cold one while we wait," said Maubi, handing me a Heineken. We drank slowly in companionable silence. "I hear they pull a body out of the sea."

"Maybe you knew her," I said. "She was a homeless person they called the spitter."

"I know she, but not by any name. Before the storm she sat along the boardwalk at night with some old book, pretending she could read when she as ignorant as the day she was born. But she was a sly one, that girl, tiefin' me twice when my back turned. She gone, good riddance." Maubi nodded emphatically, indicating the subject was closed.

Suddenly the air—which had been stilled since the storm—was filled with the roar of engines from a squadron of big-bellied military transport planes. Maubi and I stared at the sky, then turned to each other with broad grins and clinked our bottles.

Help had come to St. Chris at last.

Chapter
25

MICHAEL WAS ON the air when I left for Sea Breezes. I promised to bring him a plate of whatever was on the menu.

Margo was sitting on the balcony of her apartment with her feet up on the railing. "Kel, I've never been so damned tired in my life. I spent most of the day hauling buckets of water up two flights of stairs. You know I love you like a sister, but if you gotta pee, go outside and use the bushes."

I handed her a bottle of wine. "It's red, goes with anything and tastes better at room temperature."

She waved airily toward the kitchen. "Grab some glasses from the cupboard; the corkscrew is in the drawer next to the sink. I'm too pooped to move."

I poured us each a glass and left the corked bottle on the counter to take to the beach when we went down for dinner.

"Kel, how in the hell are you managing with power and water at home? I haven't even asked. Is your house okay?"

"The driveway's gone, and the gallery went bush, but everything else is fine."

"Is Minx all right?"

"Great. She was getting a little stir-crazy at the station. I think she's glad to be home again. When the market opens, she's getting the biggest piece of fresh tuna you've ever seen. I wouldn't have made it through the storm without her."

"Tell me what happened. Jerry said Michael broke his ankle."

"Yeah. Men. He had to do the macho thing of going out to the tower during the eye. He never came back. I thought I would go out of my mind."

"Kel, do you hate me for not being here?"

"What an odd question. Why do you ask?"

"Jerry and Abby are acting funny. Like I'm not a member of the gang anymore because I took off. I guess I've got a case of survivor guilt."

"Margo, that's the dumbest thing I ever heard. How was Bonaire?"

"Okay in a pinch, but I wouldn't want to live there. It's flat as a pancake, has more goats than cars, has more flamingos than people and most of the island is a salt flat. But the water is gorgeous. Too bad I'm not a scuba diver—I would have had a great time. Paul loved it."

"Sweetie, it's not your fault you weren't here."

"I know." Margo sighed. "Tell me about Gilda. I've never been through a hurricane."

I sipped my wine and thought for a minute. "It was worse than I expected. And I never thought it would go on so long. I think the wind was the worst part. It was like a person. A person who wouldn't stop screaming. After the eye, I thought it would begin to ease up, but it just seemed to get louder and more intense. I can still hear that sound in my dreams."

Margo reached over to hold my hand. "Tell me about Minx," she said, in a quiet, soothing voice.

"Minx freaked out a bit before the eye. I think the pressure got to her. After Michael left, I was alone in the studio. Minx jumped up on the console and stayed within petting distance, stroking my arm with her paw. When I wasn't on the phone trying to reach Michael, I'd pat her head and rub her fur." I began to laugh.

"What's so funny?"

"The litter box."

"What about it?"

"I had to pee . . ."

"Kel, with you that's an ongoing event. You always have to pee."

"I tried to leave the studio for the loo, and Minx sprang at me. She hissed and wouldn't let me out of the room. I was so desperate I peed in her litter box."

"You're kidding!"

"Well, I did shake it afterward to freshen it."

Margo began to laugh. "Then what happened?"

"The storm finally let up and Minx went to use the box for the first time. She stood next to it and sniffed. Like this." I wrinkled my nose and sniffed loudly three times. Sniff. Sniff. Sniff.

Margo set her wineglass on the floor to keep from knocking it over, and clutched her stomach.

"Then Minx glared at me. And refused to use the box. She waited until she could go outside. I've never been so insulted in my life."

I thought Margo was going to roll off her chair onto the floor.

"Kel, that's the funniest story I've ever heard."

"Oh yeah? Wait until you hear this one." I told her about Michael and the National Guard.

While Margo recovered her composure, I refilled our wineglasses.

"You know, Kel, a litter box isn't a bad idea. It's a hell of a lot easier than hauling buckets of water for flushing. Guys can always piss in the sink, but I'll be damned if I'm hopping up on a countertop to pee."

"Are you moving back here?"

"I think so. Jerry and Heidi have been great about putting us up, but I don't want to impose. I want to sleep in my own bed. It's kind of fun being here. Everyone goes down for dips in the ocean to cool off, and we've all put our perishables—the food that hasn't already spoiled—in Mitch's refrigerator. It reminds me of summer camp. Let's go down and see what's for dinner. I'll leave a note for Paul."

We took our flashlights and the wine and headed for the beach.

Mitch had set up barbeque grills for corn and chicken at five dollars a plate. I handed him half my cash for two dinners and settled down on a blanket with Margo to eat under the stars. Citronella candles, in small metal buckets the size of toddler's beach pails, were scattered around the beach to provide additional light and keep the no-see-ums and mosquitoes from eating us as we ate our food.

Paul arrived just as we finished our meal. In the candlelight I could see his face was drawn.

"I need a drink. There was a shooting at the airport this afternoon." He bent to kiss Margo hello, then turned and headed for the bar.

Chapter
26

"THAT'S THE SECOND death this week," I said to Margo while we waited for Paul.

"Who else died?" asked Margo. "Jerry didn't say anything to me, and you know how he loves to gossip."

"The spitter was found in the ocean Wednesday afternoon," I replied.

"You're kidding."

"I was there when the body was brought to shore. We all were. I was at Jerry's, and he spotted the rescue through his binoculars. Jerry, Abby and I went tearing down to the waterfront and got there as the boat was coming back. You wouldn't believe the stench from that body. It was so bad I tossed my cookies in the ocean."

"Jesus, Kel. Do you think the storm did her in?"

"Nope. The back of her skull was bashed in."

"What's one less homeless person? There will be plenty more to take her place. Have you seen some of the zombies walking around town these days? A bunch of zonked-out druggies looking for handouts to get a fix. I've been hit up for money every time I've walked down Kongens Gade. I think it's disgusting."

Paul returned with his drink to join us on the blanket. The two allotted cubes bobbed in his glass like pygmy icebergs.

"Aren't you eating?" asked Margo.

"Mitch is cooking more chicken." He paused for a gulp of scotch.

"Honey, tell us what happened at the airport."

"I wasn't in the terminal at the time—I was in the hangar checking the maintenance log. By the time the weather cleared, it was too late for me to get off the ground and back before curfew, and I didn't want to spend another night in the San Juan roach motel."

He stopped for another gulp of scotch.

"Tempers were flaring all day. When the military finally landed, I thought the mob would attack the planes. It was worse than the fall of Saigon." Paul sighed and drained his drink.

Margo held up the wine bottle, Paul shook his head. She emptied the bottle into our glasses.

"Seats out were on a first-come, first-served basis, with tourists and sick people taking priority over residents. Everyone was given numbers and told to wait inside." Mitch interrupted by calling Paul over to the barbeque to pick up his dinner, then took Paul's glass back to the bar for a refill.

"Kel, doesn't that sound like *The Towering Inferno*?" Margo whispered.

Margo and I share a passion for disaster movies. We're also hot for Paul Newman and Steve McQueen.

"Right. All those crispy critters and flying Wallendas."

"Don't forget the flying crispies," she said. The first time we saw the movie together we divided the bad-guy victims into categories. We've also watched *The Poseidon*

Adventure a couple of times, but the swoon factor is lacking.

Paul returned with a heaping plate and a fresh drink. "Kel, Mitch has food set aside for Michael. He'll cook it when you're ready to go."

"Honey, I know you're hungry," said Margo, "but we're dying to hear the rest of the story. Could you talk between bites?"

Paul polished off a chicken leg and a small ear of corn while Margo and I sipped our wine, trying to stem our impatience. "When the planes landed, the crowd broke through the barriers and stormed the aircraft. A shot was heard, and a man fell to the ground."

"Who was shot?" asked Margo. "Anyone we know?"

"I think the man was the same one we saw with Leila on the ferry the night of the blue moon barbeque at Dockside. But I didn't get a good look at him then."

"My God, are you saying Christian was killed?" said Margo.

"I don't think there really is a Christian," I replied. "But if there is, he's definitely not a Danish baron."

"How do you know that?"

"Tell you later."

Margo poked me with a sharp fingernail, which meant I owed her an explanation and it had better be good, then said to Paul, "Go on, honey, what happened next?"

Paul had his mouth full of food. We waited until he swallowed.

"The only person who didn't board the plane was identified on the passenger list as C. Turnbull."

"Who in the hell is he? Leila Mae's father? Daddy dearest?" asked Margo.

"It can't have been Daddy. He's in prison." I could have bitten my tongue to shreds.

Both Margo and Paul whipped around to stare at me.

"What?" they said in unison like a Greek chorus.

"Kel, where did you ever hear that?" asked Margo.

Me and my big mouth. Abby hadn't said it was a secret, but it wasn't my news to tell. "I don't remember. Probably an island rumor. You know how people love to make things up. Forget I said anything."

I felt Margo pinch me with those sharp nails and avoided her gaze.

"Paul," I said, "I didn't mean to interrupt. Please continue."

"There isn't much more to tell," he said, rising with his empty plate. "When I got to the scene, the shooter had escaped."

"Where was Leila Mae?" I asked.

"I never saw her," Paul replied. "I don't think she was even there."

Chapter
27

I TRIED, NOT successfully, to put all thoughts of dead bodies out of my mind before I went to sleep. But it was like trying not to think about elephants, or knowing there was a carton of ice cream in my freezer begging to be devoured. I needed a diversion.

Minx lay on a pillow next to my head, licking her left paw, then rubbing it in a circular motion over her face. I reached over to scratch the special place behind her ear and felt the rasp of her sandpaper tongue on my palm. It tickled and made me laugh.

I picked up Miss Maude's book to read another chapter before I turned off my battery-operated light. I felt like a kid reading under the covers long past my bedtime. But in those childhood days my flashlight was square and Girl Scout regulation green, and I often woke with it pressed into my face.

Back to the St. Chris of 1867. It was a fine day in late October, Tuesday the twenty-ninth to be exact. The day began with a gentle rain, but the skies cleared later in the morning. At noon the merchants shut their doors and headed upstairs to their residences for the midday meal. The government officials closed their ink pots, set aside their pens and ledgers to walk home to dine. On the outlying sugar and cotton plantations, all activity ceased as the workers sought shade under tamarind and Mother Tongue trees to rest and consume their rations.

A few minutes after twelve, a sudden change in the weather occurred. The wind—which had been a gentle easterly breeze—shifted quickly to a northwesterly gale, and rain began to fall in torrents. In the Isabeya harbor, a newly arrived Venezuelan schooner was the first vessel capsized. The other ships in port—tethered to anchors dragging across the ocean floor, destroying the coral beds that held them fast—strained against their mooring lines in the storm-tossed seas like children playing a game of crack the whip.

By midafternoon the storm was at the peak of its fury. As the wind switched suddenly to the northeast, a fingerlike waterspout came down from the sky and whirled around the inner harbor like a drunken dervish. In a matter of minutes every vessel in port was sunk, destroyed or grounded.

By the following morning the storm was gone, leaving Isabeya in shambles. The stone structures including Fort Frederick, Government House, the Scale House and Customs House were still standing intact, but the residences were hard-hit, many losing their roofs. The small wooden houses on the outskirts of town suffered the worst, reduced to kindling scattered in the dirt. The owners made plans to rebuild their homes of stone.

As they had after the fire of 1764, the dispossessed town residents sought shelter in Fort Frederick. The Colonial Council joined forces with the churches to provide food and clothing to those in need.

Town merchants who relied upon gaslight to illuminate

their homes and businesses were again forced to use kerosene lamps, as the gasworks suffered extensive damage, which would take several months to repair.

One account reported that the schoolhouse on the east end was the only building on that part of St. Chris that was not damaged.

I reread that paragraph several times, shaking my head in wonder. I looked around my little house, then closed my eyes and reached out to touch the unplastered wall behind my head, my fingertips skimming across its textured surface like a blind person reading a Braille text. I was touching one of the very same schoolhouse walls that had survived the late-season hurricane of October 29, 1867. If those weathered ballast-brick-and-coral walls could endure, so could I.

Chapter
28

"KEL, YOU'RE LATE. But if you brought ice, I forgive you." Jerry reached out to help maneuver the large cooler from the back of my car. "How can those Brits down a gin and tonic without ice? It's like drinking warm after-shave." The sour expression on his face made Jerry look more like Elmer Fudd than his fancied resemblance to Sander Vanocur.

"There's good news tonight," I said with a grin. "You're in luck. I ran my generator overtime. Just for you. But, it'll cost you. A dollar a cube."

"That's profiteering! Don't you know there's a price freeze on? Hey, Michael. How's the leg?"

"Still attached to my body," said Michael, eyeing the steep ascent up Jerry's short driveway.

"Hang on, Michael," I said. "When Jerry and I get this cooler into his kitchen, you can use me as a crutch."

"That'll be a first, Mama." Michael leaned against my car to wait.

"Hi, Kel. What did you bring?" Margo called down

from the front terrace. "I brought booze and mix. And mystery meat. It's getting funky around the edges. But we'll cook it until it chars. That'll kill any germs."

Abby was the last to arrive. "Have I got good news! There are mail trucks at the post office."

I grabbed my mailbox key to run down the hill. "Hold your horses, Kel. The post office won't be open until Monday morning at ten. But they're sorting like mad."

"I hope they lose my bills," said Jerry. "Come on, guys, let's go out back. The bar's open. Kelly brought ice."

"All you brought was water?" Abby smiled as she pushed past Margo to get a drink. "Way to go, Kel. I haven't had more than one cube in anything since the storm."

I grabbed a pair of frosty beers and took one to Michael. He lay on a chaise like a Roman emperor, with his bum ankle elevated on a small pillow, quietly talking to Heidi.

"I brought clam dip," said Abby. Her specialty is a wicked clam dip that turns to dragon fire the longer it stays in your mouth. She claims it beats Chinese mustard for clearing your sinuses.

"No dip in the house," said Jerry.

"Why not?" asked Margo.

"Have you forgotten our last Christmas party? You invited a drunken ass who slopped dip all over the Persian rug. We had to ship it off-island to be cleaned."

"I paid half that cleaning bill, Jerry, but I get the message," said Margo, carefully cupping a chip loaded with dip before popping it into her mouth.

I walked over to Abby. "Can I talk to you for a sec? In private?"

"Sure, Kel. Let's go in the kitchen. I need to marinate some boneless chicken breasts. Can you believe I was dumb enough to buy five pounds of chicken when I shopped for the storm? What was I thinking? I wish I'd grabbed a case of canned tuna."

We stood at the counter while Abby mixed the marinade—a shake of this, a dollop of that, a splash of something else, my kind of cooking—in a large plastic bowl. "What's up?"

"Abby, I did something really dumb last night. I shot off my big mouth to Margo and Paul about Leila Mae's father being in prison. I never said who told me, but I could cut out my tongue. I want to apologize for violating your confidence."

"Is that all? Kel, don't beat yourself up over it. It's not a secret. His trial and conviction are matters of public record. The man is a snake. He deserves to be exposed."

"You heard about the shooting at the airport yesterday?"

"From at least five people."

"Paul said he was identified as C. Turnbull."

"That's not a name I've ever heard, and it certainly can't be Daddy. The last I heard, he was still in the slammer. Anyway, his last name is Turner. Leila Mae had him listed as next of kin on her employment form. Which is now blown to hell with the rest of my papers." Abby finished mixing her marinade and began layering chicken breasts in the bowl. "God, I miss my phone and fax. I miss those more than anything. I feel so disconnected."

"I miss a hot shower. And the sound of my wind chimes."

"I miss cable," said Margo, entering the kitchen. "And a laundry. I'm running out of underwear and towels. I don't know how I'm going to wash anything. In the bathtub? I don't think so. What are you two gossiping about?" She dipped an index finger into the marinade bowl, then licked the finger clean. "Oh, that's yummy, Abby. What's your secret ingredient?"

"I'm not telling." Abby winked at me as she covered the bowl, sliding it out of Margo's reach. "Margo, I'm glad you're here. I need to ask a favor of you. Let's go outside where it's cooler and we can talk for a minute."

I grabbed my beer and turned to head out back where Jerry was setting up the charcoal grill with Michael's coaching.

"Kel, don't leave," said Abby. "Come sit with us."

We walked outside the house and sat on the steps leading to the front gallery. From a distance we didn't look too bad, but on closer inspection we were all beginning to look a little rumpled. I was grateful for any excuse not to iron, but knew Margo would rather die than leave the house in shorts that didn't have a perfect crease.

"Margo, I wanted to ask if you and Paul would house-sit for me."

"Sure, Abby. Glad to. Where are you going?"

"Dublin. I'm leaving next week, on the fifteenth. I'll be back the beginning of November."

"Dublin?" asked Margo. "What are you going to do in Ohio for six weeks?"

"It's the middle of nowhere, Abby," I said. "And it's going to get cold. We don't do snow anymore. Remember?"

"Broaden your horizons, ladies," replied Abby, with a smile. "I'm not going to Ohio. I'm going to Ireland."

"Wow." Margo was suitably impressed.

"Abby, that's great. Take me with you," I said.

"What is this? A vacation?" asked Margo.

"Sort of," said Abby, with a twinkle in her eyes that matched the sparkle of her diamond studs. "I'm going to run the Dublin City Marathon."

It was one of those moments when you could have heard a lizard hop.

"Since when?" I asked.

"How far is that in miles?" asked Margo.

"The standard marathon distance, 26.2 miles. I've been training for it for the past six months. I started running on the beach during turtle season. It felt so good, I began getting up early to use the track at the high school. I think I can do this. I don't expect to win—I just want to finish."

"Abby, I'm awed. Bully for you." I raised my empty bottle in a toast.

"I second that, Kel." Margo raised her own glass. "Paul and I will be glad to help you out, Abby. Tell me you've got a generator and a washing machine."

"Even better—I've got a full cistern and a gas stove. The drier's electric. I unplugged it so I wouldn't use it by accident. I wouldn't run the dishwasher, either. It takes too much current."

Margo reached out to hug Abby. "Abby, you are a life-saver."

"There's one hitch."

"I don't care. I'll do anything to keep from hauling water up two flights of stairs. Name it."

"My dogs. I was going to board them, but the vet isn't taking any boarders right now. He's too busy with the animals people have left behind."

"What? Who would desert their pets?"

"Lots of people, Kel. It's really pathetic. Every day since the storm I've seen more and more strays on the roads. The vet said people are dumping cats and dogs at his door without any identification so the owners can't be traced."

"That makes me sick," I said, heading into the house for a fresh beer. "Anyone want another drink?"

I stopped when a familiar Jeep pulled up in front of Jerry's. Pete got out on the driver's side, to walk around and open the passenger door. He helped Angie out of the car. In her arms, wrapped in a light blanket, was a new-born baby.

Chapter
29

ANGIE AND THE baby were the center of attention. Jerry hauled another chaise onto the back gallery, and Heidi went to fetch some soft pillows to cushion Angie's back.

When Angie was settled with the baby cradled in her arms, Pete went back to his Jeep and returned loaded down with baby accessories. He handled a diaper bag and portable cradle with the same effortless ease he'd hauled cases of beer during our years together.

Everyone cooed and fussed, the men more than the women. The baby slept, oblivious to all the adulation.

"When did this happen? I thought you weren't due for another month," said Margo in a voice a notch above a whisper.

"I think the storm brought it on," replied Angie softly. "Pete insisted I check into the hospital before the storm hit."

"I wasn't taking any chances," Pete said. "Angie had one false alarm at Dockside the night of the barbeque. We both spent the storm at the hospital in Angie's room. Man, that was a scary place to be. But at least there were doctors and nurses on duty." He handed Angie a glass of cranberry juice, then opened a beer for himself. "She went into labor during the eye, and the baby was born the next morning."

"The baby's dressed in yellow. What is it? A boy or girl?" asked Jerry.

"A boy. We named him Peter junior," said Pete, his chest visibly expanding. He smiled at Angie, and she smiled back, smiles so intense and intimate I wanted to look anywhere but at their faces.

"Pay up, ladies. I said it would be a boy, born in September. You each owe me five bucks," said Jerry.

"Put it on my tab, Jer," I replied.

Margo added, "Whistle for it, sweetie."

"My check's in the mail," said Abby.

"Hey, Margo, where's Paul?" asked Michael.

"Somewhere between here and San Juan. The power company has him on retainer to shuttle crews back and forth. He's bringing in a group from Guam this afternoon."

"Guam? You're kidding," said Jerry.

"That's what Paul said. Their power system is like ours—antiquated. And they're used to working in the heat. There are more crews coming from Alabama, Oklahoma and Puerto Rico." Margo headed to the bar for more ice.

"I wish the insurance adjusters would get here. I can't start repairs until I've settled with the insurance company."

"What repairs? Jerry, you came through without a scratch," said Margo.

"Did not." Jerry gestured to a guest cottage on the rear of the property. "A lot of valuable stuff in there was damaged when part of the roof went. I have an inventory."

"You used to be in the business," said Abby. "If anyone

knows how to get the most out of an insurance company, it's you. What's the secret?"

"Don't settle for anything, guys, until I've looked at your claim forms," said Jerry. "Windstorm rates will go sky-high next year, but this is the first storm to hit St. Chris since 1928. The companies will be generous *this* time. Remember, you paid for it, just like unemployment. Think of a windstorm settlement as social security with a lump-sum payout."

I nodded, remembering that my monthly insurance payments were already so high that they felt like a second mortgage. As long as I was in hock to the bank, I couldn't self-insure.

Jerry flipped Margo's mystery-meat hamburger patties on the grill while Abby tended to her marinated chicken breasts. Peter Jr. woke up from his nap, crying lustily for food and diaper changing; Angie and Pete ducked into the bedroom to care for their son. Margo and I busied ourselves putting the rest of the food on the picnic table, with a supply of paper plates, paper napkins and plastic utensils. Michael and Heidi supervised from the sidelines.

Paul arrived—to jeers of "perfect timing"—when the work was done and we were taking our first bites.

That afternoon we consumed most of what remained of our once-frozen food. Sitting around Jerry's picnic table we laughed, ate and drank as if the storm had never happened. We were all too grateful to be alive for any more talk of death.

Chapter
30

MICHAEL AND I were due for a long talk. His parting words, when I dropped him at WBZE after Jerry's cookout, were: "I want to have a baby." My reply? "It'll make medical history."

A baby? Was he nuts? What is it with men and babies? I'd never changed a diaper in my life, and wasn't about to start at the ripe old age of forty-plus. Judging from his hands-off attitude toward Minx's litter box, I didn't think Michael was keen on the diaper bit either. So where was this baby talk coming from?

I spent the remaining two and a half hours of daylight doing home improvements, while trying to muffle the generator noise with foam earplugs. Minx escaped the din by scampering up the hillside into the bush. After hanging my wind chimes inside the house on nails tapped into crossbeams, I improvised outdoor lines for drying laundry and soon had clean sheets and towels flapping in the easterly breeze. I made a temporary generator housing from sections of my galvanized tin gallery roof I found scattered across my property, then went to work on my main project—the solar water heater. That one required more ingenuity. Where was my Girl Scout handbook when I really needed it?

An easy solution was to fill my hundred-foot-long green garden hose and leave it coiled in the sun, with the nozzle tightly closed, to warm like a giant s-n-a-k-e. Another was to take the gallon plastic containers I'd filled with just-in-case drinking water and put them in the yard to heat in the solar rays. If those ideas didn't work, I'd think of something else.

I turned off the generator at sunset, reveling in the quiet. I grabbed a sand chair and a cold drink and went to sit on my gallery slab to enjoy the westerly view. Minx crept down from the hills to flop beside me. I leaned back in the chair and stretched out my legs, my heels resting on the edge of the concrete. Within easy reach on my right was a glass of iced tea; Minx burrowed her face in the palm of my left hand and I lazily scratched her throat.

As we watched the sunset I noticed a few postcurfew house lights shining in the hills, powered by the incessant whine of generators sounding like an orchestra of crazed cicadas.

I thought of treating myself to a movie on video. Who knew when we'd have cable television restored? If Benjamin's predictions were accurate, I wouldn't be watching *Holiday at Pops* live on A&E at Christmas. But my bargain telly didn't have an earphone plug, so I wouldn't be able to hear the movie sound track over the generator.

I scrapped the thought of Saturday night at the movies, and decided to listen to a Deutsche Grammophon recording of Mirella Freni and Jose Carreras in *Madama Butterfly* on my battery-operated CD player, plugged into battery-operated speakers. I remembered seeing Freni as Butterfly live at the Lyric Opera of Chicago one crisp fall night. Her performance was spellbinding. It also reminded me of a fall trip to London—my butterfly trip—*Madama Butterfly* at Covent Garden, *M. Butterfly* at the Shaftesbury, and *Miss Saigon* newly opened in Drury Lane. The red *Miss Saigon* coffee mug I bought that night at the souvenir kiosk and hand-carried all the way back to St. Chris sat on a tray atop my kitchen cupboards with mugs from other shows I'd seen in London.

At that moment I wanted nothing more than to be in London in a cozy hotel room on the West End, with electric lights quietly blazing, a tub full of hot water and bath beads from the Body Shop, and a dress-circle theater ticket for an evening performance of a brand-new production. I sighed and envied Abby her trip to Dublin. How I wanted to get off the rock and away from all my storm-related problems.

When the sky was dark and I could no longer clearly see the empty glass next to me, Minx and I cautiously made our way into the house, where I turned on the battery lamps. I shy away from using kerosene lamps or candles during power outages because of the fire hazard. One night when Minx was still a kitten, she was spooked by an outside noise and took a wrong turn off the top of the refrigerator, felling a set of standard and bracket bookshelves filled with potted herbs and jars of brandy-soaked fruit. Then she skittered across my dining table, knocking an unlit kerosene lamp to the floor, where it shattered in a zillion teensy pieces, after which she ran to hide under my bed for the next three hours while I cleaned up the mess.

I loaded the first CD of *Butterfly* and while I made dinner for Minx, heard the familiar overture and opening scene with Lieutenant Pinkerton, an American Navy officer, and Goro, a Japanese marriage broker, conferring in Italian about the house Pinkerton had bought to share with his new bride.

After putting some cheese on a plate for myself and

refilling my glass with tea, I curled up on my living-room couch to listen to the rest of the opera and continue reading Miss Maude's book.

I was up to November 18, 1867, barely three weeks after the late-season hurricane.

The ships bearing Danish and American dignitaries arrived shortly after the October 29 hurricane to find St. Chris in complete disarray. The harbor was full of sunken ships; most town buildings were roofless and in various stages of repair. The once lush verdant isle had been reduced to a leafless brown landscape.

Despite the island's storm-ravaged appearance, meetings were held every afternoon at Government House to draft the terms of sale and the referendum to be presented to the St. Chris franchised voters to support or reject the transfer.

On the afternoon of November 18, 1867, Mother Nature again intervened, further delaying the transfer of St. Chris for another fifty years, long after the deaths of the original negotiators.

A few minutes before the three o'clock start of the daily negotiating session, the first of eighty-nine tremors began to rock St. Chris.

The badly frightened visitors and Isabeya residents fled to the safety of Fort Frederick where they were eyewitnesses to the most astonishing spectacle of all.

They gasped in horror and disbelief as the sea began to recede, stranding the few upright ships in the harbor, including those that had brought the Danish and American dignitaries to St. Chris.

The officers and crews aboard those ships began to scream and curse while clinging to rails and masts for support. A few sailors fell to their knees, begging God for deliverance.

The sea rushed back in a twenty-seven-foot tidal wave, washing over Papaya Quay, drowning sailors and lifting

one ship just entering the harbor to the foot of Kongens
Gade, where it rested near Government House like a toy
boat abandoned after a bathtub cruise. The wave continued past the post office as far back as Bjer Gade, two
blocks from Government House. Meanwhile, the tremors
continued steadily for twelve hours, and would be felt off
and on for several months.

Like the sinking of the *Titanic* in 1912, the earthquakes
and tsunami of November 18, 1867—still considered one
of the most consequential seismic events in the recorded
history of the Caribbean—shattered man's unquestioning
faith in a benevolent deity. In the history of St. Chris,
1867 was a year that began with a cholera epidemic, segued into hurricane season and a devastating late-season
storm, and ended with a rumble of the earth and a roar of
rushing seawater.

As Butterfly sang her poignant aria, "Un bel di," I
thought about what I'd just read. The tragedies of 1867
were meticulously reported with eyewitness accounts
from reputable sources, but one detail was missing.

I skimmed the chapters again to be sure I hadn't over-
looked anything. I was right. Nowhere was the ship that
washed up in front of Government House identified by
name or home port. Why was that fact omitted? I read the
translator's notes at the end of the book. There was no
reason given for the omission, nor any further mention of
the ship.

Another chat with Miss Maude was definitely in order.

Chapter

31

THE GENERATOR WAS running full blast when I arrived at the station at five-forty Sunday morning, but there was no answer when I called out to Michael. The scent of freshly brewed coffee meant he couldn't be far away.

The bathroom door opened, releasing billows of steam. Michael emerged, with a bath towel wrapped around his waist and a plastic trash bag covering his cast. He was drying his hair with a hand towel and didn't see me.

"Michael! What in the hell do you think you're doing?"

He looked up from under the towel. "Morning, Mama. I just had a hot shower. Man, did that feel good."

"You what?"

He walked into Mrs. H's office to dress. I followed hard on his heels.

"How long has the generator been on?"

"About an hour."

That's when I really lost it. "Goddamn it, Michael. I told you no air-conditioning and no lights. I didn't think I had to include the hot-water heater. We've got enough

fuel to keep us on the air for another week, if we're lucky.
I sunk every cent of my own cash into getting us more
fuel, and I had to beg for it. How could you waste it? I've
been sweating it out here every day and I haven't had a
hot shower in over a week."

I slammed the door to the office and went into the music room to pull albums for my show. But first I jerked
the hot-water heater plug from the wall and flipped the
breaker that controlled the lights. Michael could damn
well get dressed in the dark.

When I emerged from the studio for a midmorning pit
stop, I found a note waiting on the reception desk.

"Have gone to check some wheels with Ben. Will be
out of here this afternoon. We'll talk later. Michael."

Out of here this afternoon? What in the hell did that
mean? Was he quitting? Damn Michael. I wished with all
my heart that I had help I could count on.

There's an old saying: Be careful of what you wish for.
For you may get it.

Rick arrived on time to relieve me, and I headed out
to my car. A middle-aged man I'd never seen before,
dressed in a clean polo shirt and ironed chinos that
branded him as a new arrival, was standing at Maubi's
van sipping a cold drink.

"Morning Lady," called Maubi. "This man be waiting
to talk to you."

"Are you Kelly Ryan, the station manager? I'm Rob
Hewitt." He extended his hand. I liked his firm handshake
and the way he looked me straight in the eye. "I hear you
may be looking for a temporary jock. My license is current; here's my résumé."

"What brings you to St. Chris, Mr. Hewitt?" I glanced
at his impressive résumé, wishing I had a phone or fax to
check his Stateside references. This was one time I'd have
to go with my gut instincts.

"Call me Rob, Kelly. I'm a freelance stringer for *Time*.

Flew over yesterday to get a story on the hurricane. I like your operation. It's small, but you've got a good reputation. Henri Margeaux in St. Barts said if I got over here, I should look you up. He sends you his best."

The Associated Press stringer on St. Barts was the owner and general manager of the local radio station. I'd met Henri at Caribbean Broadcasting Association meetings and we'd become good friends. Henri was a level-headed man whose judgment I could trust.

"If you know Henri—" I said, and was interrupted by Michael's return with Benjamin. I introduced the three men. As Michael and Benjamin went into the station, Michael called to me, "I want to go over the schedule with you before you leave." I nodded and turned back to Rob.

"Come back tomorrow after twelve-thirty, and we'll talk. I may be able to use you part-time." We shook hands, and I went back into the station with Rob's résumé.

"Good news, Michael. I may have gotten some temporary help."

Michael grabbed the résumé out of my hands. "You can't hire that guy. Don't you know who he is?"

"His name is Rob Hewitt. He's got Stateside major-metro experience and knows Henri Margeaux in St. Barts. I'm in a bind here, Michael. I need help."

"I know I've been a class-A jerk, Mama, and I'm really sorry about this morning. My head was totally up my ass. But this guy is bad news. He's a shock jock who makes Stern sound as benign as the Pope. I was in Miami last year when Hewitt was bounced off the air in the middle of a broadcast. And it wasn't the first time. He hasn't worked on the air since Miami. The guy's garbage mouth cost him a cool mil a year in salary and bonuses. Sit down, and I'll tell you about it."

I listened carefully as Michael related the events of that morning in Miami. If even half of it were true, I'd narrowly escaped professional suicide.

"Jesus, Michael. I thought Hewitt's name was familiar, but I didn't make the connection. You saved my butt. Thank you. I owe you big-time."

Michael reached for my hand and held on tight. "Come on, Mama, I'll buy you lunch someplace after I pick up my new set of wheels. You deserve a break today."

"What wheels?"

"Ben ran into a guy who's leaving the island and needs some quick cash. He's got an automatic for sale cheap. I can drive as long as I don't have to shift. It's time I got my act together, Mama, and stopped being a leech. What do you say, Ben? How about some lunch?"

Benjamin had been silent the entire time Michael and I were talking. I looked at him, and saw sweat pouring off his face. His body was racked with uncontrollable chills.

"Benjamin, what's wrong with you?"

"I've got to get home. I feel like I broke every bone in my body." He rose from the chair, then crumpled to the floor. His forehead was hot enough to fry an egg.

Michael and I managed to revive Benjamin, get him in my car and drive him home. Camille and Trevor were having a picnic lunch on their gallery when we arrived.

"Camille, Benjamin's not feeling well," I said. "It came on suddenly when he was at the station. He said he feels like he broke every bone in his body."

Camille and Trevor helped get Benjamin inside and into bed. Camille popped a thermometer into his mouth. The mercury quickly shot up to 104°.

Benjamin was the first on St. Chris to come down with post-Gilda dengue fever.

Chapter
32

MICHAEL AND I took Trevor with us to give Camille a Sunday afternoon to herself.

We picked up Michael's wheels, a car of uncertain vintage that made my hatchback seem fresh-off-the-lot new. The trick to owning a car on St. Chris is not to go for the flashiest one with the most accessories. The more you add to a car is more that can go wrong, requiring extensive time in the shop for repairs and waiting for parts to arrive from the States.

Michael's car was typical island transport. It needed a paint job but had good tires, the upholstery was worn but duct tape would keep the foam from falling out, there were no visible signs of rust and it started when he turned the key in the ignition. The broad smile on Michael's face reminded me of a kid with his first jalopy. We piled in the front seat and headed toward Columbus Bay in search of a snack and a walk on the beach.

On that November day in 1493 when Columbus discovered St. Chris on his second voyage, he anchored his fleet outside the reef-protected bay that would later bear his name. The Carib Indians in residence weren't overly fond of their drop-in visitors, and the fleet soon pulled anchor to head eastward along the northern coastline toward the main harbor where the more hospitable Arawak tribe had established a small village. The Arawak settlement became the town of Isabeya, originally spelled Isabella, while Columbus Bay remained sparsely populated and was known primarily as the island hurricane hole.

We pulled up to the Columbus Bay marina where I often docked Top Banana. The palm-frond-thatched roof that covered the restaurant's terrace had gone bush, but it was the bay itself that left me speechless. Everywhere I looked were broken boat hulls smashed into the storm-twisted mangroves lining the shore.

Most of the tables were occupied by boat bums telling war stories about riding out the storm on live-aboards. Doug, the harbormaster, sat at the marina bar nursing a beer and chatting with the bartender, who was flipping burgers on a charcoal grill. In the background was the ever-present sound of generators punctuated by the occasional screech of a gas-powered chain saw.

While Michael and Trevor were looking at the wrecked boats, I walked over to the bar to talk to Doug. "Hey, Doug, how did you make out?"

"Hey yourself, Kelly. You're looking good. You doing okay?"

"Same as everyone else. Were you at Harborview during the storm? It looks like it took a beating."

"Man, that was one hairy night. Why they didn't evacuate that place before the storm beats me. I was snug in my cottage, but the people in the hotel were scared shitless. The next morning they were begging to get off the Quay and back to town."

"I saw the ferry got mashed. How did they get to shore?"

"I ran a shuttle in my inflatable dinghy. It was the only boat available. Someone stole the one from the manager's office during the storm."

"What a crappy thing to do."

"Yeah. Some of those tourists were really ugly. But they're all gone now, and the hotel is shut down for repairs. I like having the Quay to myself. You ought to come over sometime in your kayak."

Michael and Trevor came up to the bar to place their orders.

"Ready for a burger, Trevor?" asked Michael.

"I just ate lunch. My mom says I should wait for an hour before going swimming so I don't get a cramp." Trevor tugged my hand. "Miss Kelly, will you be my buddy? Dad told me never to swim by myself."

"Trevor, we forgot to bring towels."

"Here, Kelly, use mine." Doug handed me a red-and-white-striped Harborview beach towel.

"That looks brand-new," I said.

"I guess it is. The hotel bought them for the winter tourist season. But the manager cracked the boxes and gave them out to all the guests the night the storm hit. I don't think he'll be needing them now."

Michael slid onto the barstool next to Doug and ordered a beer and a burger for himself and a refill for Doug.

Trevor and I walked north along the debris-strewn beach, looking for a sandy spot where we could enter the water.

Trevor walked quietly with his head down, hunting for seashells.

"How did you make out during the storm, Trevor?"

"Okay."

"How did that baby SnakeLight work out?"

"Okay."

"Have you got enough batteries? If you run out, I've got some extras you can have."

"Okay."

We continued to walk in silence, but I could tell something was wrong.

"Trevor, look at me. Tell me what's bothering you."

When he looked up, I saw tears in his eyes. "Is my dad going to die?"

"Oh, Trevor, no. He's not going to die. Come sit with me on that log." We walked a few feet inland to sit side by side on a piece of driftwood. "Why would you ask such a question?"

"My dad never gets sick. I heard him tell my mom one time that if he was ever sick enough to stay in bed, she'd better call the undertaker."

"Trevor, he was just teasing. He didn't mean it." I put my arm around Trevor and held him close. I felt his tears soak through my T-shirt to my skin. "Honey, your dad's got dengue. Do you know what that is?"

Trevor shook his head, rubbing his runny nose against my shoulder.

"You get it from mosquito bites. You don't know you have it right away, it takes a few days. Then you feel pretty awful for a while and everything hurts. You sleep a lot, but you get better and soon you're okay again."

"How do you know that?"

"Because I had it one time after we'd had a lot of rain. I was at the supermarket on a Saturday morning, when suddenly I felt so awful I had to leave my cart in the middle of the aisle and go home."

"What did you do?"

"I went to bed and stayed there for ten days until I got better."

"Who took care of you?"

"I took care of myself."

Trevor put his arms around my neck. "If you get sick again, Miss Kelly, you call me. I'll come over to your house and make you some soup. Do you have a microwave? My mom lets me make soup in the microwave all the time. And I'll read you a story. My dad always reads to me when I'm sick, and it makes me feel better."

I hugged Trevor and wiped his nose with the hem of my shirt. "Okay now? Let's go swimming." Trevor and I splashed in the tepid ocean until almost three. "Are you ready for a burger? We have to hurry so Michael can get to work on time."

"I'm not really hungry. Can you take me home now? I want to make some soup for my dad, and then I'm going to read him a story from my new *Star Trek* book."

We ran back to the marina. When we dropped Trevor at home, Miss Maude was sitting on the gallery talking to Camille. I made plans to visit with Miss Maude the following afternoon.

Chapter
33

THE FIRST OF the small miracles that would restore our lives to a semblance of normalcy came on Monday with the arrival of the mail truck.

I hauled the bundles of a week's worth of mail into the studio and began sorting. Junk into the wastebasket, bills and anything that looked like checks went into a stack to be opened later, magazines were piled to haul into the office. I immediately opened an envelope addressed in a familiar scrawl—how could I not recognize the little circles masquerading as dots over the i's?—postmarked San Juan a few days earlier.

Dear Kelly,

I'm stuck in San Juan and can't get back to St. Chris. I'm going to Los Angeles to meet grandmother's cruise ship when she comes home on the 15th.

I hope you're okay.

Love, Emily

Damn. I was counting on Emily to come back and take over her receptionist duties. Not that there were any phones to answer, but we were behind on billing and log sheets and all the detail work of running a radio station. It looked like I'd have to work on playing catch-up during my airtime. I wanted to wring her irresponsible neck.

But, before noon, one of my other defectors returned to work. Cass, one of my two afternoon regulars, was back on the job. I quickly rearranged the schedule. Cass would be on the air weekdays from noon to four. Rick was back on the weekend shift and, if he wanted it, could have weekday work on the computer helping me with paperwork.

I waited until twelve-forty-five, but Rob Hewitt never showed. Which saved me from having to tell him I had no openings after all. I made a note on my calendar to chat with Henri Margeaux at the next Caribbean Broadcaster's meeting.

Feeling more on top of things at WBZE, I headed for Miss Maude's to try to solve a mystery.

We spent the afternoon going through the leather-bound volumes in her father's library, stopping every so often for iced tea breaks on the gallery. Our search proved fruitless.

"After the transfer in 1917, most of the government records were taken to the Danish National Archives at the Castle of Copenhagen," said Miss Maude. "I know my friend is a dedicated researcher. If there was any public information on that ship, he would have included it in his account. Unfortunately for historians, many of the colonial records are not accessible by the public." She put the last book back on the shelf and locked the glass doors of the cabinet. "I shall continue looking through Papa's library, but I don't think we'll have much luck."

I wished I had brought the spitter's coin, but that could wait for another time. I left Miss Maude to head for home and stopped in town when I remembered I hadn't picked up the mail from my own post office box.

The stamp and package window was already shut for the day, but the main doors were still open. In my mail was the usual assortment of bills and circulars, and an appeal from the Red Cross for donations to help those victimized by Hurricane Gilda. I snorted and tossed the letter in the trash.

Four-thirty. An hour and a half before curfew. I had time to run to Dockside for a quick visit with Victoria.

Her office door was locked. A neatly lettered sign read "No rooms available. Manager on duty from ten to noon, six to eight. Leave messages in the box at reception." I headed back down the brick staircase and stopped at the foot of the stairs.

The last time I saw the spitter alive was the morning after the storm. I sat on the bottom step, closed my eyes and tried to remember what I'd seen.

Was it only a week ago? I had trouble remembering yesterday. Every day since Gilda was a day spent coping with one damned problem after another. Days that all seemed to blend into one.

I got up and walked to the place where I'd been standing that morning. I'd come down Kongens Gade and stood looking at the harbor, at the gazebo bandstand where the remains of the cabin cruiser were still impaled, then at the boardwalk. The spitter had come from the direction of the Watering Hole and vanished from view near the Dockside staircase.

I walked back to the stairs. They were solidly built of ballast brick, protruding at a right angle from the stone building. There were no niches, no hiding places that I could see. Perhaps it had just been my imagination. But where had the spitter been during the storm?

I had just enough time to get home before curfew. I raced home to feed Minx and spent the rest of the evening with a flashlight, Caribbean history books, paper and pen cil. I crawled in bed, with Minx one leap behind me, reread a slim volume on Danish colonial architecture had bought at a flea market for fifty cents when I wa remodeling my schoolhouse. In it were detailed drawing of all the old buildings in Isabeya. But they didn't gi me any clues to where the spitter might have holed during the storm.

Chapter
34

THE NEXT AFTERNOON I headed to my car as soon as my shift was over. I had my hand on the door handle when I spotted a folded piece of paper stuck under my windshield wiper.

The note read: "Kel, I want to talk to you before I leave. Can you meet me at my office when you're off the air? I'll supply lunch. Abby."

I drove to town and parked in the fort parking lot. As I walked past the Watering Hole, I spotted Carole sweeping up storm debris.

"Carole!" She put down the broom and we hugged. "It's so good to see you. How did you make out?"

"Oh, Kel. Isn't this a mess? We're hoping to reopen the end of this week, but I don't know how we're going to make it. There's so much to be done."

"How are you going to manage without power?"

"We've got a gas stove and a generator to run the refrigerator/freezer. The menu will be limited to hot dogs and hamburgers. We'll only be open for lunch until we get power and the curfew's lifted."

I looked around the courtyard. "It won't be the same without the round table. I suppose it got smashed to bits."

"Didn't Jerry tell you? He hauled it into the real estate office. It's over there at Island Palms along with the yellow umbrella and all those tatty captain's chairs you guys love. You don't think Jerry would let his investment go to waste, do you? What did you guys pay for that table?"

"Fifty bucks, six years ago. I think we got the chairs tossed in for nothing. I remember Jerry hit us up for ten dollars each to pay for it."

"I can't wait until we reopen. I'll be glad to get out of the house."

"Is everything okay at home, Carole?"

"Same as everyone else. No power, and we lost part of the roof, so we're living in the downstairs apartment. We had it rented to one of the new schoolteachers, but she left on the first plane out of here."

"How are your kids?"

"Driving me nuts." Carole smiled. "They should be back in school by now and out of my hair. Summer vacation was long enough. Did you hear about the spitter?"

"I was there when they brought her in."

"Kel, is it true? Was she murdered?"

"Where did you hear that?"

"It's all over the island."

"I wish the storm had killed her." I clapped my hand over my mouth. "Carole, I don't know why I said that. I wasn't wishing her dead."

"I know what you mean. She was a pain in the ass, but she didn't deserve to die." Carole looked around the deserted restaurant. "Kelly, can you keep a secret? If this gets out, it'll cost me my job."

"My lips are sealed. Cross my heart."

"The spitter was here during the storm."

"How do you know?"

"Because I let her in. She showed up Sunday when I

was closing up before curfew. Kel, she was really pathetic. She had a couple of plastic grocery bags with her. I think that was everything she owned. I tried to talk her into going to the shelter at the Anglican church. I said I'd drop her off on my way home. But all she did was shake her head and point to the bathroom."

"Is that where she usually spent the night?"

"No. And that's why the boss insists we keep it locked. He doesn't want it trashed by vagrants or druggies."

"I wonder where she usually slept?"

"Somewhere close to the fort, I think. I saw her hanging around the gazebo a couple of nights when I was closing up at the Lower Deck. For all I know she slept at the top of the library steps."

"You work here and at the Lower Deck?"

"I've got two boys in junior high. They grow out of tennis shoes before I'm finished paying for the last pair. I help out at Dockside whenever Victoria is shorthanded."

"What did you do about the spitter?"

"I unlocked the bathroom door and let her in. I showed her how to lock and unlock the door from the inside, and I gave her some food and water and our emergency flashlight. Then I left for home. I never saw her again."

"You did the right thing," I said. "She wouldn't have survived if she'd had to fend for herself."

"But she didn't survive, did she?" Carole looked close to tears.

"You have nothing to blame yourself for. I'll tell you something. I saw her right after the storm, and she was still alive."

"What happened to her?"

"I don't know, Carole, but I'm trying to find out."

"She left her grocery bags in the john," said Carole. "I found them when I was able to get back into town to check on her. Kel, do me a favor and take them. I don't want to throw them away, but I can't keep them here. I don't want anyone to find out what I did."

"I promise you, it'll be our secret."

I followed Carole down the outside steps to the area behind the kitchen where the bathroom and storage area were located. The spitter had good instincts—the women's loo was as snug and safe as a bomb shelter. Carole unlocked the storage-room door and hauled out a knot-tied black trash bag.

"I don't know what's in there, and I don't ever want to know," said Carole, handing me the bag. "I'll always feel guilty I didn't take her to the shelter. She might still be alive."

"I'll take it to my car now," I said, lifting the slippery plastic bag, which was surprisingly heavy. I cradled it in my arms like schoolgirls used to carry their books before backpacks. "If you see Abby, tell her I forgot to stop at the post office and I'll be right back."

I dumped the bag behind the front seat of my car, then ran across the street to the post office to buy some stamps before the window closed for the day.

Abby was waiting, in what remained of her office, with a small cooler. A blue FEMA tarp covered the missing section of roof, the afternoon sun making the room look like we were at the bottom of the cobalt sea, but everything inside smelled like a swamp. Abby's office furniture was stacked along the walls, and rolled area rugs stood on end in the doorway.

We ate our lunch on the second-floor landing in front of her office door, sitting with our bare feet dangling over the edge like kids on a summer-camp pier. Abby brought sandwiches, a slightly stale bag of chips, and canned, pre-sweetened, lemon-flavored tea.

"Jerry said he'd get the rugs to Paul to ship off-island to be cleaned. I should have thought to roll them in plastic before the storm, but who knew? I never expected the roof to go. Thank God for insurance."

"Amen, sister." I raised my tea can, then slurped.

"And computer backups. Barbara is already working at home to reconstruct my files."

"I backed up the WBZE stuff before the storm hit. Then unplugged the office computer so it wouldn't get fried."

Abby put down the last quarter of her ham and cheese on rye. "Kel, I wanted to talk to you, in private, about Leila Mae. I thought she'd be long gone, but she's still hanging around. I spotted her this morning walking into the pharmacy. That red hair is hard to miss. Lord knows why she hasn't left, but she can't be up to anything good. I shouldn't say this when you're stuck here on the rock, but I can't wait to get out of here."

"Put me in your carry-on, Abby. I won't take up much room." We both smiled. "I've brought you something for luck." I removed a plaited leather thong from around my neck and handed it to her. "My grandmother brought this with her from her native Ireland."

Abby looked at the stone suspended from the thong. "What is it? What does it do?"

"It's a luck stone, made of Kilkenny marble. Don't ask me to pronounce its name in Gaelic. Granny said in Ireland everyone carried a stone with a hole in it for luck. When she was safely home, it always hung over her bed. Here's the best part." I took the stone from Abby's hand and held it up to my eye. "Granny always told me—" I did my best to mimic my grandmother's brogue— " 'Kelly, me darlin', if anyone should ever look upon you with the evil eye, you look right back at them through the hole in this stone. It'll take away any harm they might wish you.' Then Granny would laugh, hug me and slip me a sweet from her pocket."

Abby slipped the thong over her head, and held the stone up to her eye, looking like she was sporting a monocle. "Kel, that's a great story. I would have loved know-ing your grandmother. Thanks. I'll take good care of it and bring it back to you. Where was your grandmother from?"

"A little village in County Galway. She emigrated when she was a young woman. Lucky for me she missed crossing on the *Titanic* by two days."

"You're kidding."

"It's a family legend. A week before Granny was due to leave her village, she came down very suddenly with a terrible fever and was confined to her bed. She hoped that because of the coal strike the *Titanic*'s crossing would be delayed. But when she arrived in Queenstown on April 13, the *Titanic* had sailed on schedule two days earlier. Granny always said it was the luck stone that saved her life. Wear it in good health, Abby."

Abby smiled, then became as serious as if she were delivering a closing argument.

"Kel, I really need to talk to you about Leila Mae. I don't think you understand how truly vicious and evil she is. I'm going to tell you what she did to me. And this is strictly between us, okay? Please don't tell Margo or Jerry."

Abby turned to face me, sitting cross-legged with her elbows resting on her knees. "A few days before I caught Leila Mae boffing Pete on my office couch, I had a call from a client. A sweet little old woman who never cheated anyone in her life. I'd taken care of a small matter for her and billed her a modest amount, which she paid by check. She was calling to tell me that when the check came back from the bank, it had been altered to read one hundred and fifty dollars, instead of the fifty dollars she'd been billed and paid. She was very apologetic about it, but thought I'd want to know."

My eyebrows flew over the rim of my sunglasses. Abby nodded.

"I checked my desk calendar. I was off-island the day the deposit was made. I looked at my checkbook. Only fifty dollars was shown as going into the account. I had four more calls from clients with similar stories. When I finally received my own bank statement, after Leila Mae was gone from St. Chris, there was a check made out to cash for five hundred dollars. A check I'd never written."

"Son of a bitch."

"I called other people Leila Mae had worked for. They all said the same thing, but no one could prove it. So, they trumped up an excuse and fired her. Just as I did when I caught her with Pete."

"Jesus, Abby. What did you do?"

"I made good on the money to my clients, referred the matter to the bar association and the attorney general's office, and hoped my law practice hadn't gone down the drain. If I don't get away from here and the sight of that damned woman, I won't be responsible for my actions. She poisons the air we breathe." There was a wan smile on Abby's face, but no laughter in her eyes. "I want you to keep something for me, Kel." Abby went into the office and returned to the doorway, holding an oblong metal box.

"What's in there?"

"Come in the office and I'll show you."

We went back inside with the remains of our lunch. She unlocked the box. Inside the box was a gun.

I stepped backward. "Oh my God. Abby, is that yours?"

"Of course it's mine, Kel. Don't be such a ninny. You're not afraid of guns, are you?"

"Only if they're loaded and pointing at me," I said, remembering a winter evening in Chicago when I was held up by two men at gunpoint a few feet from the entrance to my apartment building. That night I ran, screaming obscenities at the top of my lungs, and was safely inside my apartment before the perps knew what had happened. A few seconds later a plainclothes cop was knocking at my door and the perps were spread-eagled against the unmarked squad. I was very lucky that night, as only the young and feckless can be.

"This .38's not loaded, Kel. There's a box of ammo in there as well. I want you to keep it for me. Please? Put it in your floor safe. I can't leave it here and don't want to leave it at home, and the banks are still closed so I can't get to my safe-deposit box." Abby closed and locked the gun box, sliding it into a canvas tote.

I reluctantly took the tote from her hands.

"I owe you, Kel. I'll bring you something very nice from Ireland."

Chapter
35

I DROVE HOME as if the hounds of hell were on my tail. I don't think I drew a deep breath until Abby's box was secure in my floor safe, hidden under my wooden jewelry chests.

The sun was over the yardarm somewhere in the world, which definitely made it drink time at Casa Kelly. I mixed a gin and tonic, treating myself to lots of ice and one of the last of my home-grown key limes, and went to sit on the gallery slab. While there was still daylight, I wanted to explore the contents of the spitter's sack. I went back in the kitchen for a pair of disposable rubber gloves.

The spitter hadn't left much of a legacy. In the first bag were a couple of T-shirts, some gray underwear that had once been white but washed with not enough soap and no bleach, a cast-off pair of Reeboks with the name "Robert" lettered in indelible ink on the tongues, a cardigan sweater missing most of its buttons, and a torn plastic rain poncho mended with duct tape. Wrapped in a threadbare towel were a pink toothbrush with splayed bristles, a collapsible plastic cup like one I had at summer camp, a sliver of soap and a comb. I imagined her using the clothing for a pillow and the poncho for a blanket.

In the second bag was the item that gave the sack its weight. A leather-bound volume with covers that felt, even through rubber gloves, like the finest suede. Marble-patterned endpapers and pages of finely lined paper so beautiful it would be sacrilege to deface them with as crass a writing instrument as a ballpoint pen. On the fly-leaf, written in ink turned sepia with age by an educated hand schooled in the art of penmanship, were the words: Niels Larsen, Customs Controller, St. Cristofero, Danish West Indies, 1867.

Minx butted her head into my thigh. How long she'd been sitting next to me, I had no idea. But her message was clear. Dinner. Now.

After finding no personal identification of any sort other than the name inked on the tennis shoes, I rebagged the spitter's clothes, saving them in a plastic storage box with a tight-fitting lid. For what, I didn't know, but like Carole said, it didn't seem right to abandon her skimpy wardrobe to the refuse heap. Not until I'd talked to Benjamin. However, that little chat would have to wait. Miss Maude said Benjamin was out of it, sleeping twelve to eighteen hours a day, and feeling awful. "Breakbone fever is what they call it, Kelly. And for quite good reason." When I had dengue, even my eyebrows hurt. I knew just how bad Benjamin felt.

I went back to the gallery with a fresh drink and the ledger. How had the spitter ever gotten her hands on it? It belonged in the library's Caribbean collection, or in the Castle at Copenhagen in the Danish colonial archives. But there was no way I was letting it slip out of my clutches. I held the book to my face and sniffed it, the way a man sometimes sniffs a shirt to see if it will stand one more wearing before being tossed in the laundry hamper. The scent was book lover's Chanel No. 5. A heady bouquet of paper and leather, with a musty undertone that gave me a sense memory of being deep inside an Egyptian pyramid, and a hint of citrus. Probably from the oil residue on my fingertips after squeezing the lime for my drink.

I turned to the first page and began to read. The text was mostly in English, the common spoken and written language taught in the St. Chris schools throughout the Danish colonial period and used in official correspondence. The tracts I'd seen in Miss Maude's library setting forth Danish laws for the West Indies were printed in Denmark in both English and Danish.

As I read, I quickly discovered that the book was a private journal, not an official record. But that still didn't explain how it had ended up in the spitter's possession.

The first entry was dated Sunday, October 13, 1867. After a brief description of the sunny, clear weather and a mention of the full moon, Larsen noted: "I am in receipt of a private communication under Royal Seal from Denmark, dated August last, concerning the dispatch of a shipment from Copenhagen, that I dare not mention by name, for fear of my life if this should fall into unfriendly hands. But it will greatly ease the monetary crisis that affects our island, as we have been reduced to scrip which has no value beyond our shores. I am instructed to remain at my post, day and night, from early November onward until it is safely received and secured. How shall I explain to my wife and young son my prolonged absence, though our house in Isabeya be but a short walk away?"

I skimmed the next few entries, stopping at the one dated Tuesday, October 29, 1867. "The time is nearing for me to take up residence in the Customs House. The day began with a small rain, but looks to be clear for the balance. I now take myself home for the midday meal with my family. How I shall miss this simple pleasure in the long days and nights to come."

The next entry was dated Friday, November 1, 1867. "I had scarcely reached my home on the Tuesday last, when a drastic change in the weather occurred. We were seated at our dinner table when the storm came upon us. The wind, which throughout the morning had been blowing from its usual easterly direction, took a sudden turn to the N.W., bringing upon us a frightful gale which lasted until late in the evening. Midafternoon, as we sought shelter within the confines of the house, after having—praise be the strength of Almighty God—secured the shutters and doors at considerable risk to life and limb, the wind stopped as if a candle flame had been extinguished in one breath, then quickly came again from the S.E. I have heard tell, but did not witness firsthand, the terrible fury of the tornado that rendered our fine harbor a graveyard of ships and men. Of my own dwelling, little remains that is habitable. I have dispatched my wife and son to the country to reside with her brother on his cotton estate until our house can be repaired and have taken up my own residence in a small room in the Customs House. Many of our townspeople are now quartered in Fort Frederick until their own dwellings are once again fit to inhabit. I fear for the ships at sea.

"Sunday, November 3, 1867. It has only been a matter of days, but I yearn for the comfort and company of my family. I pass the long lonely nights at the sea-view window, looking through my glass for the signal I have been told to expect. There is great activity in the harbor as it must be cleared to afford passage for the ships arriving soon with dignitaries sent here to discuss the sale of this very island upon which we live. Perhaps the recent hurricane is a blessing to us from Divine Providence to keep this island under Danish rule.

"Monday, November 11, 1867. We did not clear the harbor in time to allow close anchorage, but the passage through the reef was unblocked by the time the warships bearing the dignitaries arrived yesterday afternoon and this morning. The men and their aides were escorted to Government House, where there are dry beds for all. With the injury to the gas house we are once again dependent upon kerosene lamps and candles for illumination and I fear those to be in short supply. There is still no sight of the ship I seek. I spoke with both captains of the newly arrived vessels and learned of the misfortunes which have struck our neighbors to the north as a result of the storm. The Danish captain was more forthcoming, as we were able to speak in our native tongue, and he confided to me the dire tales told to him of pirate vessels which are known to traffic in our waters, bringing fear and trepidation to the hearts of the honest men they plunder.

"Tuesday, November 19, 1867. As is my usual practice, on the day before I write this account, I had partaken of the midday meal, followed by an hour of rest and a brisk walk through town to rid me of my lethargy, and was climbing the stone steps of the Customs House when I felt the steps begin to tremble. I fell to my knees and quickly navigated the few remaining steps to the upper landing and thence to the confines of my office. The trembling continued with such force and fury that I feared for my life and escaped from my office to the safety of the nearby fort. It was as if the very hand of the Lord God Almighty had been afflicted with a palsy, so the earth did shake. As to what followed soon thereafter, I do not have the proper words to tell of such a sight that had naught been seen by the eyes of mortal man. It was as if a soup basin had been tilted askew, so did the mighty sea depart our shores, leaving exposed the rocky bottom whereupon lay the wreckage of the ships laid waste by the recent storm. The reef that secures our harbor was bared to the midafternoon sun. As quickly as the sea left us, so did it return in a mountain of water, carrying with it all it had taken and more."

I quickly turned the page to continue reading Larsen's account of the 1867 earthquake and tsunami, but the remaining pages were blank.

Chapter
36

I LEFT THE journal face open on the gallery slab in the afternoon sun while I went to the kitchen side of the house to fire up my charcoal grill for dinner.

Normally I find waiting for coals a waste of time and prefer using my portable gas grill, but I had one steak left in my freezer and wanted it cooked to perfection. That meant charred on the outside, medium rare inside, seasoned with freshly ground pepper and a dash of garlic salt. My mouth was already watering, but it would be worth the wait. I wrapped a potato in foil to bake in the coals and searched my cupboards for anything else I might cook as long as I had fire. Coffee-can stew, a throwback to my Girl Scout camp outs, came to mind. But I didn't drink coffee, and had no ground beef or vegetables to make a stew. I didn't even have the ingredients to make s'mores or angels on horseback. I hoped the supermarket would reopen soon. In another day or two, Minx and I would both be eating canned tuna. The very thought made me gag.

When the charcoal lighter had done its job and the coals were slowing turning white, I returned to the gallery. I gasped in dismay when I saw what had happened to the priceless book I'd left unattended. The pristine blank pages now appeared foxed and blotched. Miss Maude would have hung me by my thumbs or gone to the cane field in search of a supple switch. I sighed and picked up the book, mentally kicking myself for being so careless. When I was five years old I received my first library card, and I still remember the red-lettered stickers pasted in the front of all the primary grade books: Please Wash Your Hands Before Reading This Book. I also remembered the time I was expelled from the library for a week for giggling during story hour.

I looked at Larsen's journal, wondering how I could undo the damage. But the damage had been done long ago by Mr. Larsen himself. What appeared to be age spots were actually words, faintly inscribed on the facing pages. I held the open book close to my nose and sniffed, and again smelled a whiff of lime like the West Indian lime cologne—imported from St. John in its distinctive wicker-caned bottle—that I wore every day. But this time my hands were clean. I'd washed them in my kitchen sink after starting the fire. The whiff of lime came from the pages themselves.

I carried the journal into the house and left it open on my dining table while I ransacked my shelves for a book on codes and ciphers. I opened it to the chapter on steganography: concealing the presence of secret messages. Skimming the historical section describing tattooing shaved heads, then letting the hair grow back to conceal the message, I soon found the section on invisible inks.

Invisible inks are generally divided into two types: chemical and organic. Not believing for a minute that Mr. Larsen had immediate access to a chemistry set, I skipped ahead to the organic. Milk, vinegar, onion and lemon juices were commonly used by the Arabs as invisible inks as far back as 600 C.E. What was good enough then was good enough in 1867 on a tropical island where small key limes grew wild.

Gentle heat was the key to revealing the hidden message. I turned to the remaining pages, but they were still blank. What I needed was a hair dryer, but I hadn't owned a hair dryer since the old bonnet style was popular in the late sixties. When I chopped my waist-length hair into a pixie cut I threw away every hair accessory but a brush. What else could I use? Gentle heat, the book said. A heater? Who had one of those in the tropics? Wait a minute. I had a heater in my car. Of course I'd never used it and wasn't sure it even worked. And probably shouldn't waste the gas when the filling stations were still closed and I was down to less than half a tank. That left an iron or a lightbulb.

I cranked up the generator and dug my iron out of its hiding place in the kitchen pantry. Forget the ironing board—it was wedged behind my stepladder and vacuum cleaner. When anything I owned needed pressing, I generally used a folded beach towel. I turned the iron to its lowest setting. While I waited for it to heat, I went back outside to check the coals and broil my steak.

I licked my index finger to test the iron. After hearing a faint sizzle, I carefully held the iron over the blank pages, moving it slowly back and forth to distribute the heat evenly. Letter by letter, word by word, Mr. Larsen's secrets were at last revealed.

My steak grew cold and the butter congealed on my baked potato as I devoured Larsen's account of a sailing ship swept ashore by a monstrous wave, the fate of the men who sailed her and what became of the priceless cargo secreted beneath her decks.

But whether these tales of pirates, false flags and buried treasure were facts chronicled by a rational man or fiction created by a brain fevered with tropical disease, only time would tell.

Chapter
37

WHEN I FINISHED my shift on Wednesday I headed to town to pay Victoria a visit, arriving at Dockside as she was locking her office shortly after twelve.

"Kelly, how lovely to see a friendly face. Let's sit someplace cool where we can put our feet up. Would you like a glass of tea?"

Victoria and I passed the unoccupied reception desk on the way to the Posh Nosh bar. The tables in the elegant restaurant were covered with chairs turned upside down instead of the usual freshly ironed linen tablecloths. The mahogany bar, normally filled with thirsty lunch guests waiting for a table on a midweek workday, was empty. In place of the impeccably dressed bartender in a spotless long-sleeved, open-collared white shirt and black vest were an assortment of liquor bottles, a supply of plastic glasses, small bottles of mix, a pitcher of tea, an ice bucket and an honor-system money box. Victoria poured us each a glass of tea, then picked up a liquor bottle. "A spot of rum to sweeten your tea?"

I raised my hand with thumb and index fingers so close together they were practically touching. "A microdot."

Victoria added a generous tipple to her own glass, then passed the bottle to me. "I've been dealing with the insurance man all morning. You can't imagine how grueling it all is," she said, sighing. "Come. Let's get out of this gloomy place and sit on the back terrace." She waved her hand in the direction of the Lower Deck. "I can't bear looking at that debris one more minute."

"Why don't you have it hauled away?"

"I can't until the insurance man is through with his blasted paperwork. It's all too, too tiresome."

We settled ourselves on chaise lounges.

"Have you got any guests?" I asked.

"I'm full up at the present. But it's all the power crews, and they're away from the hotel from sunrise until curfew. They're quite a jolly lot. Very good about tidying up after themselves and not demanding clean sheets and towels every day. I haven't the staff or the facilities to cope with that. So far only my cook and two of my maids have come back to work. How are you managing?"

"About the same. All but one of my disk jockeys have finally come back. I may actually have a weekend all to myself without having to work. These seven-day work weeks are wearing."

Victoria eyed me over the rim of her glass. "Is this a social visit?"

I smiled. "Yes and no. I hate to bring up a sore subject. Have you solved your mortgage problem?"

"Not yet. I'm hoping for a quick settlement with the insurance company. That would allow me to pay off the mortgage before the demand date. Then I could seek alternate financing for the storm repairs. It's all very nip and tuck at the moment. What with Abby taking off on holiday and the banks still closed. . . . I can't even phone or cable my solicitor in London. But why do you ask?"

"Vic, I can't say anything right now, but I have a question. Do you have any building plans for the hotel?"

"I'm afraid I don't follow you. Do you mean what am I going to do about repairing the damage?"

"No, Vic. I mean blueprints, architect's plans. Photographs. Sketches. The older the better."

"It's odd you should ask. The only blueprints are quite recent, done up a year ago when I was thinking of adding more rooms. But only last night I was going through the files in storage, looking for some papers the insurance man wanted, and I ran across an old scrapbook a previous owner compiled. I have it in the office. Let's go have a look, over another glass of tea."

We headed back to the bar for refills. This time I took a pass on the rum. I'm a cheap drunk, especially on rum. All that sugar goes zipping through my system like a bullet. We went into Victoria's office and locked the door behind us.

She opened her filing cabinet and handed me a photo album—the old-fashioned kind with stiff covers joined with a long cord like a shoelace running through the holes in the black-paper pages. The photos and clippings had been lovingly placed into black corner mounts, reminding me of tiny embossed arrowheads. The descriptions and dates beneath each picture were written by hand in white ink.

We paged through the album together. "Vic, look. There's Miss Maude and Miss Lucinda. Oh, how young they are. I wonder if the men with them are their husbands. That must be Miss Maude's daughter. Wasn't she lovely? You know, she died several years ago in Denmark." We turned the pages. In one photo I thought I recognized a smiling Benjamin with his classmates. Benjamin at the same age Trevor was now. And a much younger Maubi, grinning as he sat astride the roof with a hammer in his hand. When we finally reached the last page, I turned to Victoria. "Would you mind if I borrowed this? I'm sure Miss Maude would love to see it. I promise to take good care of it." Which meant I wouldn't leave it on my gallery unattended or anyplace Minx could get at it with her claws.

Victoria wrapped the album in a plastic trash bag and secured it with tape, then slipped it into a shopping bag.

"How long has this been a hotel?" I asked.

"Almost fifty years. It opened after the war, when tourism was just beginning. About the time the present airport was built."

"What was it before then?"

"Nothing, really. An abandoned building, I think. I was told it suffered extensive damage during the 1928 hurricane, and was finally sold for back taxes in the late forties."

"Vic, how well do you know your insurance man?"

"Mr. Prescott? I've known him as long as I've owned the hotel. He's the local representative for Lloyd's of London. Why?"

"I just wondered. He should be able to push through your settlement in no time at all."

"Oh, but I'm not dealing with Mr. Prescott. He took ill a few days after the storm and sent an independent adjuster in his place. Wait, I've got his card right here." I sat patiently, sipping my tea while Victoria thumbed through her papers. "How odd. I know he gave me his card."

"What was his name?"

A funny look crossed Victoria's face. "I can't remember. It must be the heat. I find that happening quite often recently. I'll head off someplace, then stop because I can't remember where I'm going or what I need to do when I get there."

I reached out to touch Victoria's arm. "You're stressed out, Vic. We all are. Gilda turned our lives inside out.

Can you tell me what the man looked like?"

"Oh, yes. He's quite dapper. An older man. Been in the business for many years, he said. The poor thing told me he took a nasty tumble in San Juan. He slipped on the tarmac before getting on the plane and injured his arm."

A warning bell began clanging in my head. "Vic, I know you need the money badly, and you're in a hurry to get it. But do me a favor. Wait for Mr. Prescott to settle your claim. Deal only with people you know and trust."

"Well, all right. If you say so. But why, Kelly?"

"Did you ever read Margaret Mitchell's *Gone with the Wind?*"

"Many years ago. After the war. When I was a teenager in public school in Kent."

"You might want to read it again. Vic, the carpetbaggers are here, and I'm afraid they're out to fleece us."

I left Victoria in her office, pouring over insurance papers. I decided to drive up the hill to Jerry's house on my way home, but remembered he was working on disaster relief at Government House.

It would be a kick to see Jerry really working for a change. Instead of hoofing it to the fort parking lot, I turned right onto Kongens Gade and crossed over to Government House.

Finding Jerry wasn't difficult. I followed the queue to the former stables, where the meeting had been held the day before the storm, which now served as Jerry's command post. Instead of the sound of water splashing merrily in the courtyard fountain, I heard the clatter of manual typewriters. The fountain was stilled, and the water had turned a murky pea-soup green. It looked as off-putting as most of the island swimming pools, now the color of lime Jell-O and used mostly as water reservoirs for flushing toilets.

"Kel, do you need a loan or did you come to volunteer?" Jerry waved to me from a desk in the back of the room.

"Actually I came to watch you work." I sat in his visitor's chair, put my elbows on his desk and rested my chin on my interlaced fingers, gazing at him adoringly.

"Get out of here, Kel, you're embarrassing me." Jerry laughed and swatted at me with his clipboard.

"Sorry, sweetie. There is something I need. Do you have a list of insurance adjusters?"

"Sure. But I told you I'd take care of checking your paperwork."

"It's for a friend."

Jerry called across the room to a harried woman busy interviewing a grant applicant. "Where did we put the adjuster list?"

"In the file on your desk with the blue tab," she yelled back over her shoulder.

Jerry shuffled through the folders piled on his desk. "I've got three files with blue tabs."

"Look inside them."

Jerry finally found the correct file. "Here you go." He handed me a mimeographed list that smelled like a second-grade spelling test. "We're trying to conserve power. Someone found an old duplicating machine in one of the back rooms with a box of stencils and a case of fluid."

"Definitely a pre-Columbian artifact. You could put it in Fort Frederick museum. Tell me, what do you have to do to get on this list?"

"You have to be licensed to do business in St. Chris."

"And how do you do that?"

"You fill out a form and pay a fee."

"So anyone can become an approved adjuster?"

"Not anymore. Only if you qualified before the storm. There have been no new applications taken since then.

Tell your friend to watch out; there are flocks of vultures on the streets looking for fresh meat."

"Thanks, Jer. I hear the Watering Hole may reopen the end of this week. I'll buy you a white on white on the rocks when it does."

Jerry smiled like a cat dreaming about a saucer of cream.

I trotted back to Dockside to show the list to Victoria. "Do you recognize any of these names?"

Victoria studied the list carefully. "No." She closed her eyes and thought for a minute. "I just remembered his name. Carl Turnbull." She looked at the sheet of paper again. "He's not listed. Thanks for tipping me the wink, Kelly. I'll be out of the office the next time he shows up. Now I think I'll pay a call on Mr. Prescott. I have a jar of calves' foot jelly from Fortnum's that should put him right as ninepence."

I walked to my car, smiling to myself as I remembered the first rule of a good con: Never change your initials. Leila Mae hadn't married a Danish baron, that I knew for a fact; but she'd definitely found a man to equal dear old Dad.

Chapter
38

COLUMBUS DISCOVERED OUR tiny island during his second voyage in 1493. After planting the flag of Spain and dispensing a few trinkets—mostly beads made of glass— to the awestruck Arawak Indians, he departed the newly christened Isabella for points north, and did not return to St. Chris until his fourth voyage in 1502. Columbus believed that he had discovered a new route to Asia; but not until the Portuguese seafarer Vasco da Gama traveled to India in 1498 by going eastward around the Cape of Good Hope was a distinction made between the East and West Indies.

Columbus was a man who knew the value of publicity. Word of his exploits spread throughout Europe, inspiring Pope Alexander VI, father of Cesare and Lucrezia Borgia, to issue a proclamation in 1493 dividing the newly discovered Indies between Spain and Portugal. Which was all very well and good—unless you happened to be French, Dutch or English.

By 1506 the French Sea Wolves were whizzing around

it reached the open water, the flag was soon struck. For the six weeks the ship spent at sea, whenever another vessel was sighted, the tricolor was raised and all precautions were taken to conceal the true origin of the Danish ship, as once the fearsome Teach did strive to confound his enemies. I am at a loss as to what to do with the concealed cargo, as the intended destination was rendered unsafe by the dreadful storm and made more precarious by the recent earthquake. I have not the time to await new orders from Denmark. The representatives of the King have left our shores on a ship that arrived last evening, so quickly did they depart that the anchor was barely wet when it was raised. I pray the Almighty will guide me in the decision that I alone must make.

"Monday, November 25, 1867. We have worked long these last two nights under the merciful eye of darkness as the new moon is fast upon us. The cargo is safely stowed. As long as mortal man may tread upon our shores, his eyes shall never see it. I raise my goblet to the success of our labors. Vive la France.

"Wednesday, November 27, 1867. Captain Thorsen passed to his eternal reward this morning after a rapid onslaught of fever. I fear I too shall soon join him and pray to Almighty God to keep my beloved wife and son from this calamity. I leave behind this token so they will know my chronicle to be true, and my time away from them not to have been spent in idleness, but in the devoted service of His Majesty, King Christian of Denmark. I remain, until death, his obedient servant."

Following Larsen's final entry was an impression the size of a dime. I held the book close to my face and saw, pressed into the fibers of the paper, an image of a field of sugarcane. The paper around it was blotched by an oily stain, looking as if it had been made by the tallow from a dripping candle.

Chapter
39

MY PLANS FOR Thursday afternoon were knocked out of the water by a flyby visit from Margo as I was getting ready to leave the station.

"Kel, get your butt in gear," she yelled through her open car window. "There's something really big going on in town."

"The Watering Hole opened a day early?"

"Better than that."

"What's better than food?"

"Money, honey. The bank reopened this morning at ten, and it's closing for the day at two."

"Tell me this is for real. I'm down to my last nickel."

"Get a move on, Kel. They're only letting five people in at a time, and the line is already halfway around the block."

"You go ahead. I need to grab the station deposit. I'll meet you there."

"I'll save you a place in line. We can talk then." Margo slid her foot from the brake to the gas pedal, then eased into the bumper-to-bumper traffic crawling toward town.

Life in St. Chris after Gilda was one continuous queue, and standing in line at the lumberyard, fuel depot, pharmacy or bank had become a bonding ritual as strangers traded storm stories and tips for survival and parted company new best friends. I already had enough "what do to with canned tuna" recipes to fill a two-volume cookbook.

"How are you making out at Abby's?" I asked, as Margo and I inched our way forward. We were five feet away from the shady side of the building, with only a hundred people ahead of us in line, and I couldn't wait to get out of the sun. Margo was clever enough to have thought of wearing a wide-brimmed straw hat, but my head was bare, and the sweat was dripping like a leaky faucet off my hair and into my eyes and ears.

"Just great. I can't tell you what a relief it is not to haul water. You know, if I didn't hate yardwork so much, I'd be looking for a house to buy. There are a lot of bargains on the market right now. Can you believe I'm actually busy at the office taking new listings? The Continentals are fleeing and grabbing any offer they can get. One woman told me she couldn't wait to move to Florida."

"Good choice. Everyone knows there are never any hurricanes in Florida."

Margo smiled and fanned her face with her hand. "How about you and Michael coming over for dinner Saturday night? Abby said we should eat anything we find in the freezer that's not green and dancing. I saw a guy standing next to a truck on the side of the road this morning. He had live lobsters for sale. I could stop on the way home and ask him to get us four for Saturday night. How about it? Steamed lobster with oodles of melted butter and garlic bread sound good to you?"

"I drool at the thought, but we can't—there's still curfew."

"Oh, damn. I keep forgetting about curfew. I'm so sick of curfew I could scream."

"Amen, sister," came a voice from behind us in the line. Margo turned and smiled. The speaker smiled and waved. Instant bonding.

"Okay, Kel. Here's plan B. You and Michael come for dinner and spend the night. Abby's got a guest room, and I know she won't mind."

"Sounds good to me, sweetie. I'll leave a note for Michael at the station tomorrow."

"A note? Kel, that's so high school. Like passing notes in study hall or dropping a note in someone's locker between classes. Aren't you two talking?"

"We're on different shifts. He's at home while I'm at work, and when he's at work I'm home and it's curfew."

"Maybe you two should move in together."

"Let's not go there, Margo."

"Why not? Kel, is everything all right? The last time the four of us had dinner, Friday night before the storm, you two were tight as ticks."

"Margo, you're from New York. No one says 'tight as ticks' in New York."

Margo shrugged. "You're right. That's vamp of Savannah talk. Is that bitch still around? I haven't laid eyes on her since the day we flew home from San Juan and she tried to bribe Paul into getting her tail out of here. I hope she finally got her round heels off St. Chris."

"Abby said she saw her heading into the pharmacy earlier this week."

"Oh damn. I wonder what Leila Mae's up to now. Whatever it is, it's going to be trouble for someone. What's the line from Cervantes? 'Whether the stone hits the pitcher, or the pitcher hits the stone' . . ."

We finished in unison: "It's going to be bad for the pitcher." We raised our arms high and smacked hands like players on a basketball court.

I opened my mouth to tell Margo about the time I played Dulcinea in *Man of La Mancha*—when I still had waist-length hair and a voice that could reach the high notes—for six weeks in dinner theater and how the actor playing Don Quixote ate onions before every performance and I got back at him with garlic but clamped it shut again. The less said the better. My show-biz past was a secret I intended to keep. In a deeply religious community like St. Chris it wouldn't do for the gossipmongers to know I once stood naked on stage eight performances a week in the cast of *Hair*. It could cost WBZE advertising revenue and me my job.

"Margo, do you remember who Leila Mae worked for the last time she was here?"

"Honey, I barely remember yesterday, and you want me to go back five years? Let me think for a minute." She fanned her face and thought. "I'm sure this isn't a complete résumé. She seemed to change jobs every two seconds. Is it possible she was only here six months?"

"And that was six months too long."

Margo nodded. "You got that right. I think she worked at the bank, then the title company, or maybe it was the other way around. But who really cares? I know she tended bar for a bit at the Watering Hole. That's when we met her, remember? And then she worked for Abby. After that, she was gone. I might have missed one or two brief encounters—she went through jobs like men—but I think that's pretty much it. Why?"

"Just curious."

"I think there was one point when she was studying for her real-estate license, but she never took the test. Let's not talk about her anymore. It gives me a headache."

By the time we got out of the bank it was almost two. Even though cash withdrawals were limited to three hundred dollars per day per account, I had money in my wallet again and enough ready cash from the station account to pay for the next load of generator fuel. We were down to our last half tank, which made the fuel depot the next stop on my list.

"Kel, where are you headed? Got time for a drink? We can go over to Sea Breezes and get one from Mitch at Port in a Storm. I need to pick up some clothes from the condo."

"Sweetie, I'll have to take a rain check. I need to order more fuel for the station. If the generator goes dry, we're SOL and OTA."

"Kel, there are times I wish you'd stop talking in jargon. I need my Orphan Annie decoder ring to figure out what in the hell you're saying."

I opened my mouth, but Margo waved away my explanation.

"Kel, I'm teasing, I know what you meant. Don't forget lunch tomorrow at the Watering Hole. Jerry moved our table and chairs outside this morning. We're having a ceremony to raise the yellow umbrella at twelve-thirty sharp. Be there or be square."

"Wouldn't miss it. I owe Jerry a drink."

Margo danced sideways in the direction of her car. "Sweetie, I'm out of here. I've really got to pee, and there are no loos open anywhere in town. Tomorrow. Watering Hole. 'Bye."

I got into my car, which in spite of the sunshade covering the front window was hot enough inside to roast a small chicken, and drove to the fuel depot, where I stood in the broiling sun for another hour waiting to get to the front door. By the time I paid for the Friday fuel delivery my mouth was so dry I could grow cactus in it, and my head was splitting. I've never had heatstroke and didn't want to find out firsthand what it felt like. Instead of stopping at WBZE to chat with Michael about Saturday night dinner, I headed home for a cool drink and a cold shower.

Chapter
40

WHEN I ARRIVED at the station Friday morning, I found a note from Michael propped on the studio console.

"Gone to San Juan for the weekend to get my leg checked and cast changed. Back Monday in time for my shift at four. Cass will work for me Friday night and Rick will fill the afternoon slot for Cass. It's cool, Mama. Don't get your knickers in a twist. Michael."

Why did I have the feeling the inmates were running the asylum?

And why was nagging jealousy eating away at me because practically everyone I knew was getting off the rock for R & R and I was stuck minding the store? Whine, whine, whine. I laughed myself out of my snit by reminding myself it was lonely at the top. I decided I would head out in Top Banana early Saturday morning for some fun of my own. If the seas were calm.

I went into the music library to pull albums for my show. I was looking for something cheerful by Mozart, perhaps a hornpipe concerto. Obviously I had sailors and pirates embedded in my brain. Thinking of Mozart reminded me of a lecture by one of my music professors at Northwestern when he described little Wolfgang as the Salzburgian Shirley Temple. The image of a child prodigy tap-dancing his way to the piano made me smile.

Flipping through the *M*s, I ran across a Broadway's Greatest Hits album featuring Mary Martin. I turned it over to scan the contents and liner notes. Everyone remembers Mary Martin in *Peter Pan, South Pacific* and the *Sound of Music*, but the show that propelled her to early stardom was *Leave It to Me*, in which she sang Cole Porter's "My Heart Belongs to Daddy." I hummed a few bars, put the album back on the shelf and continued looking for Mozart. I gave up looking for the hornpipe music—the actual title of the piece eluded me—and picked out an album of three quartets and *Eine Kleine Nachtmusik* for the morning classics.

I turned on the computer and began paperwork while the music aired. Now that the post office and bank were open again, I had to get caught up on the accounting and billing.

When Mozart ended, I went on the air with a brief news summary. There wasn't much news to tell. A very short list of who was open for business; a progress report on the restoration of power and phone service, which could have been summarized as "don't get your hopes up"; a reminder about curfew; and a rehash of tropical weather cribbed from the BBC. "Highs in the mid to upper eighties, low near seventy-five, calm seas with easterly swells one to two feet, chance of rain twenty percent today, tonight and tomorrow." Same old, same old.

After the news I switched to Leonard Bernstein conducting the New York Philharmonic in a recording of Gershwin's *Rhapsody in Blue* and *An American in Paris*. Oh, how I wanted to be in Paris. Or I wanted to be Leslie Caron dancing with Gene Kelly in Paris.

I was caught up on the accounting by the time Rick arrived for his four-hour stint. As I left the station, heading to the Watering Hole for the first lunch since Gilda, I realized it was also the first weekend since the storm that I didn't have work. What was I going to do with all that free time?

The Watering Hole was jammed with customers filling every table. The round table was back in its usual spot; I snagged my favorite chair, one with a small gouge in the right arm but with sturdy legs that didn't wobble.

"Don't sit down yet, Kel," said Jerry. "We're waiting on Margo."

Margo was panting when she reached the table. "Sorry I'm late. Traffic was a bitch, and you don't want to know where I had to park. But I brought something special to mark the occasion." She reached into her bag for a small brown envelope. "I had these made in a little shop in Bonaire." She handed each of us a small brass plaque, engraved with our names. "No more fighting over chairs, guys."

I quickly put my name on the back of my chair before Jerry could grab it for himself.

"Abby and Pete can pick their own. After all, we're the regulars who paid for this table in the first place. I had three more made that say 'reserved' for any strays who show up." She tore the paper backing off a larger sign that also read 'reserved' and stuck it in the middle of the table.

"Can we cut the gab and get on with it?" Margo and I imitated buglers playing reveille while Jerry cranked open the umbrella. Everyone applauded.

"First round's on me," I said, as Carole came to take our orders.

"It's hot dogs or hamburgers, with or without cheese. Choice of chips, potato salad or coleslaw. I wouldn't dawdle, the burgers are going fast. All the condiments are on a table next to the grill. Now, what'll you have to drink?"

Jerry ordered his usual white on white, Margo and I opted for gin and tonics.

Jerry got up to table-hop, like a politician glad-handing for votes.

"Are we on for dinner tomorrow night, Kel?" asked Margo.

"Michael took off for San Juan for the weekend," I replied.

"Oh? What's in San Juan?"

"His note said he was going over to get his cast changed."

"Well, you come anyway. I found the lobster man and ordered four. They're ten dollars each. If he can't get them, we'll grill whatever's left in Abby's freezer. Then we can watch movies on video. It'll be fun, Kel."

"Sounds good to me." I dug in my purse and handed Margo twenty dollars for my share of the lobsters. "I'll bring a couple of bottles of wine. Red or white?"

"White with seafood, I think." Margo laughed. "What am I saying? It's not as if we have many choices these days. Who can afford to be picky? Kel, bring whatever you've got. It'll be perfect. If the supermarket were open, I'd beg for one of your key lime pies."

I smiled. "Say please."

"Kel, are you holding out on me? Do you know something I don't? Is the market open?"

"Not that I've heard. But I do have a pie in my freezer, or the chill box I call my freezer, and if it's edible, it's yours. I made two the last time we had dinner and stashed the extra one."

Margo reached over to hug me. "You are a wonder. And a hoarder. Come early. We can watch a movie in the afternoon before Paul gets home, then have dinner, and see another movie before we go to sleep. What time can you get to Abby's?"

"I'm going out in Top Banana in the morning. I need some R & R."

"I'll expect you around two. And if you're not there by three, I'm sending Abby's dogs out for you and that key lime pie." She glanced over at Island Palms Real Estate, where a couple stood reading the listings posted on the door. "I smell a commission. Be right back."

I sat by myself at the round table, looking down the palm-tree-lined cobblestone walkway toward the seaside boardwalk that skirted downtown Isabeya. It was almost three weeks from the day Margo, Abby and I sat at the round table having lunch and complaining about the heat. The palm trees were standing tall, as they had for decades, even though they were missing most of their fronds. Those would grow again. The cobblestones, laid when the flag of Denmark flew over St. Chris, would still be there when we were dust. The battered buildings would sprout new roofs as they had after storms in the past; the harbor would once again be cleared of wreckage and the board-walk rebuilt. Life would go on. That is the lesson that history teaches us.

I felt a curious sense of continuity with Niels Larsen, the customs inspector. But was I clever enough to follow the trail of clues he left behind? Little did I know that I was involved in a race to the finish that would nearly cost me my life.

Chapter
41

THE CLOUDLESS SKY was still ablaze with stars when I shoved off in Top Banana into an ocean calmer than I'd ever seen it. If I looked hard enough I could see faint pinpricks of light reflected in its mirrored surface.

Directly overhead Orion marched toward the west, followed by the Gemini twins, Castor and Pollox. Ahead of me, a few degrees above the eastern horizon, Venus shown like a beacon.

I looked at the shore, where Minx sat stiffly at attention with her striped tail curled tightly around the right side of her body, with only the very tip quivering nervously like a snake's rattles. Her pose reminded me of the life-size granite statue of the Egyptian cat god Bast, one I'd bargained for in a small market on the west bank of the Nile across from Aswan, which now resided on an end table in my living room.

"Go home, Minx. Don't you know we're violating curfew?" Minx ignored me. "Go home!" She ambled a few feet inland to the high-tide line, turned toward the sea and lowered her belly onto the cool damp sand, looking like a small sphinx awaiting the sunrise.

Minx would find her way home again when she was good and ready. We'd walked the quarter mile from my house to the inlet where I kept Top Banana moored, so I wouldn't be caught driving during curfew on a day when I wasn't on my way to work. To me, walking in my own neighborhood was a minor violation and one I easily shrugged off.

I was traveling light on this excursion. Orange nylon shorts and a ratty old T-shirt, surf mocs on my feet, sunglasses, visor and my key ring clipped to a lanyard around my neck and tucked inside my shirt. My only cargo was a bottle of water and my kayak paddle.

As I paddled against the gentle current toward Venus, the still-moonless night reminded me of accounts I'd read of the *Titanic*'s sinking. The sea as calm as glass, stars reflected in the water. Because of Granny's near miss in sailing on her, I'd been fascinated by the ship since I was a small child. I'd once gone to Liverpool to see an exhibit of *Titanic* artifacts, and spent an hour by myself in a small, dark curtained room where a model of the foundering ship was enclosed in a glass case.

Surrounding the lighted ship were tiny lifeboats, and overhead twinkle lights arranged into constellations provided the only illumination for the exhibit. I bent my knees until my eyes were level with the waterline and duck-walked slowly around and around the case, listening to the taped voice of Second Officer Charles Lightoller recount the events of that tragic night. It still gives me shivers.

I dipped my hand into the ocean to test the water temperature and wiggled my fingers, creating shimmers of phosphorescence in the sea like an underwater aurora borealis. The water was still warm enough to bathe in.

Because of the easterly trade winds and westward-flowing current, I'd never taken the eastern route along the St. Chris shoreline. I admit it, I'm a lazy paddler. I like as much help from nature as I can get. I usually dock my boat on the sand when I've traveled as far west as I care to go, then drive to pick it up later and haul it back to its mooring place. But on a morning with no wind and a flat sea, I felt like exploring new territory and would let nature carry me home when I reached my turnaround point.

Top Banana moved through the water like a hot knife through butter. I watched the sky lighten from cobalt to purple, then to pink tinged with gold, and listened to the sugar birds twittering on shore. A few brown fronds hung, bent or broken by the storm, from the coconut palms and would soon fall to the sand below.

The homes scattered along the sparsely populated shore had not fared well. Not one had a roof and none were covered by tarps, which told me the owners had either fled St. Chris or were snowbirds who had not yet returned. I passed one dwelling that was wind-stripped to bare walls and empty window frames, and wondered if its front door was still locked.

The docks were reduced to listing pilings, and I paddled out and around them to avoid any debris in the shallows. The sun had risen, making it impossible to see what was under the water ahead of me.

A leisurely twenty-minute paddle ahead of me, I spotted the entrance to a cove and decided to head for shore. I needed to make a pit stop.

After I pulled Top Banana onto the beach and was looking for a discreet place to pee, I was surprised to see signs of recent digging in the storm-flattened remnants of cotton plants that had once been widely cultivated on land unfit for sugarcane.

I looked around but didn't see or hear anyone. I moved closer to examine the site. There was a hole that looked about four by four by four, a size that would comfortably hold the antique wooden poultry seed box I used at home to store linens. If I jumped in the hole—which I wasn't about to do under any circumstances—my armpits would be almost level with the ground.

Why would anyone be digging in such a remote spot on the east end? The area wasn't accessible by car. The paved east-end road curved inland a mile or so east of my house and then headed west along the southern shore to form a loop back to Isabeya. Whoever had been in this spot had arrived on foot using the overgrown estate boundary paths or journeyed, as I had, by sea.

All I could think of was Jerry saying he wanted to be the next Mel Fisher. Yo, ho, ho and a bottle of St. Chris rum for you, Jerry, I thought, laughing to myself. It would be just like Jerry to go out with a shovel to dig for buried treasure. Except he'd want to lime in the shade directing the operation while someone else did the real work.

Something sticking in the dirt at the bottom of the hole glinted in the sunlight.

I leaned closer, but my body cast a shadow in the hole. I moved to the far side to get a better look.

There was definitely something down there, and it looked like the edge of a gold coin.

I lay on my tummy in the dirt—feeling like Minx cooling her belly in the sand—with my legs flat out behind me, and stretched my arm into the hole as far as I could reach. Who did I think I was kidding?

The only way I was going to get whatever was in the hole was to get into the hole myself.

Never say never, I muttered, as I tested the ground to make sure the sides of the hole would hold my weight when I wanted to get out. I took off my right shoe and stuck it in my waistband.

I eased myself into the hole and picked up the object with my toes. I bent my right knee and raised my leg until

I could grasp the coin with my fingers. My high-school dance coach would have been proud of me.

The coin in my hand was slightly smaller than a nickel and looked so new it could have been minted in Denmark yesterday. The obverse bore a right-facing profile of a man. Above it the words "Christian IX, 1867, Konge Af Danmark." On the reverse, circling a three-masted ship under full sail, were the words "20 Daler/1920 skilling— Dansk Vestindien."

I wanted to sit down in the hole and scream, like a kid who's had his unwrapped lollipop snatched from his grasp.

How had anyone gotten to Larsen's treasure ahead of me?

I remembered Maubi saying he'd seen the spitter sitting on the boardwalk before the storm, night after night, pretending to read an old book. If Maubi had seen her, odds were that others had as well.

Was I the one being taken for a ride by a phony treasure scam? Was Larsen's journal a fake? Or was Larsen himself deluded? His mind maddened by the fever that claimed his life? Did Niels Larsen ever really exist?

Like an idiot, I'd forgotten to wear my watch. But looking at the sun's position in the sky I figured it was somewhere between ten and eleven, and if I hauled ass for home, I'd have a chance to get to Miss Maude's before I was due to meet Margo.

I pulled my shoe out of my waistband, put the coin in the toe under the liner, slipped the shoe back on my foot and faced my next challenge. How in the hell was I going to get myself out of this damned hole?

By the time I emerged, my clothes were sweat-soaked and covered with dirt. My shoulders ached, and I felt like my elbows and wrists were going to snap. I headed toward the ocean for a quick dip before getting into Top Banana to paddle home.

I'd taken only a few steps when I felt a sharp blow on the back of my head and fell face forward in the dirt and sand.

Chapter
42

"DADDY, I TOLD you we should have dropped her in that hole and buried her. Bringing her on board was a dumb idea."

"Leila, honey, we've made more than one mistake already. We can't afford another one. We'll get rid of her the way we did the last one."

"That stupid homeless woman? If she'd given me what I wanted, I never would have hit her with the brick. All I wanted was that old book she carried around. But she pulled the bathroom door shut behind her, grabbed the beach towel off my head and started running for the boardwalk. I had no choice but to go after her. She would have ruined our entire plan."

"Leila, the hurricane ruined our plan. We should have left the minute we heard it was coming."

"It was too late. I'd already made such a fuss inviting everyone to my party, I had to go through with it. It was a good idea, too. One of your best. The coins were real works of art. They would have fooled anyone. Those stupid people on St. Chris would have coughed up a fortune to be part of a treasure hunt. Do you know how much Mel Fisher got out of his investors?"

"But he spent it all looking for real treasure. Which he finally found. There are always other islands, sugar."

"Let's get moving. I want to be docked at one of them by dark. This time I hope you get into deeper water. No more of this shallow stuff. That's where we messed up last time."

"We'll go out beyond the reef. Give me that nautical chart hanging on the wall."

There was the sound of a clipboard thumped on a countertop.

The distant sounds came into my head as if they were filtered through bales of cotton. I lay facedown on a bunk, on top of a rough blanket that tickled my nose. My head hurt so damned much that if I moved it even a fraction of an inch I knew I would throw up. My queasy stomach was further agitated by the idling boat slowly rocking from side to side.

"Daddy, stop wasting time and get us out of here."

"In a minute, sugar. There should be a cut in the reef along here somewhere. But it's not marked on the chart."

"Screw the damned chart."

"Leila, if we don't find the cut, we have to go all the way to Isabeya to pass through into the open ocean. I'd rather not have this boat seen by anyone who can identify it later."

"Have it your way."

"You look for the cut. You said you knew where it was."

"That was five years ago. The storm changed everything. Where are the binoculars?"

"Inside the cabin where you left them."

I heard footsteps overhead and closed my eyes.

"No, they're not. Daddy, they're right here. You must have moved them."

"Well? Where is it? Where is the cut?"

"I can't see anything, Daddy. The sun's in my eyes."

"You take the wheel. I'll look."

A brief silence, then: "Five hundred yards ahead. Slow down, Leila. If you go through too fast, you'll rupture the gas tanks."

I felt the boat slowly turn to starboard. And after a few seconds, a faint scraping—as if an emery board had been slowly pulled across a ragged fingernail.

"Good girl. Now head due north. In five minutes we'll be in the Puerto Rican trench. The chart says it's the deepest water in the Atlantic Ocean, almost as deep as Everest is high."

"What a great place to dump that goody-two-shoes bitch. I always hated her. The night she threw champagne in my face at Harborview, I wanted to kill her on the spot."

"You keep going, I'll bring her up top."

This time the footsteps came down the stairs and over to the bunk. I kept my eyes closed and felt myself being carried across the small room and up the stairs. My head banged against the hatch and in spite of my resolve, my stomach heaved.

I threw up all over the front of Daddy's clean white shirt.

It was then I heard Leila Mae say the three little words that will haunt my dreams for the rest of my life.

"Dump her overboard."

Chapter
43

I HIT THE water with a splash. When I surfaced I looked up to see heading away from me a black leviathan with the name *Gotcha* painted in gold script upon the stern.

I spent the next few minutes treading water until the boat was out of sight. In the distance I could still hear the faint roar of its engines.

The penny finally dropped when I found myself humming "My Heart Belongs to Daddy."

How could we all have been so blind? The true love of Leila Mae's life was, and always had been, dear, dear Daddy. Whether he called himself Turner, Thorsen, or Turnbull didn't really matter. Abby was right. They were a pair of snakes.

I was swimming in water the color of a midnight blue sapphire. Water so deep there would never be a bottom. It scared the hell out of me. I wanted to jump skyward, like a kid trying to see over a wall, to get a visual fix on the St. Chris coastline, but the sea gave me no leverage. Behind me I heard the *Gotcha*'s engines rise in pitch. The sound kept moving away from me and gradually faded to nothing.

I felt the gentle sea swells push against my back and let them carry me forward. Waves always head for shore, I said to myself over and over, certain I'd read that somewhere but knew I'd probably made it up. There was no signpost to measure my progress. Only the sun slipping off to my right gave me a sense of direction.

It was time to take inventory. I was still dressed in my shorts, T-shirt and surf shoes. My sunglasses had slipped down around my throat when I hit the water. I pushed them back up over my nose and secured the safety strap behind my head. The lanyard hung around my neck and by some miracle my keys were tapping against my chest. Only my visor was missing.

Someone will come looking for me. I kept repeating that to myself like a mantra. But who? Only Margo knew I was going out kayaking, and I had no idea what had become of Top Banana. Where would she look? At my house? The inlet where I usually tied up my boat? No one would ever think to look for me in the middle of the Caribbean Sea. And if they did, no one would ever be able to see me, a tiny dark-haired speck on the water. I needed to do something to make myself visible.

Grabbing my waistband with my left hand and vowing not to let go no matter what, I pulled my knees close to my chest in a tuck position and carefully peeled my orange-nylon shorts over my shoes.

Then, I slid the waistband over my head. The wide leg opening acted like a hood, giving me temporary shade from the burning sun. I soon gave that up as a bad idea, fearing that a sudden wave would come up from behind and carry the shorts away, leaving me completely invisible. I slipped my head through the leg and wore the shorts around my neck, hanging down my back like a cheap lei.

I have no idea how long I was in the water, only that

the sun was moving farther and farther to my right. I thought I saw a faint speck of green on the horizon but discounted it as a mirage. Or wishful thinking.

The thought of spending the night floating in the open ocean terrified me.

I tried not to think about the ravenous sea creatures down there, somewhere underneath my feet.

I tried not to think about the *Titanic* passengers in that frigid below-freezing water, clinging to bits of wreckage before dying of exposure.

I tried not to think about the spitter. Dead from a blow to the back of the head before she hit the water.

I tried not to think how my body would smell if I died at sea and was found adrift after several days.

I tried not to think about Minx, keeping vigil on the beach.

I tried not to think. Period.

I was moving along—half-floating, half-swimming—in a semiconscious state, when I felt a faint shudder. Like a tiny shock wave deep beneath my feet.

Please God. Not sharks. Don't let it be sharks.

I whipped my head from side to side, but saw no telltale gray fins circling in the water.

Then, the sea began to move. I felt myself pushed backward, as if someone had fired a cannonball at my stomach.

I rose higher and higher and saw the reef outside Papaya Quay coming at me with incredible speed.

I took a deep breath, then clamped my hands over my mouth, pinching my nose shut with my fingers, and squeezed my eyes tightly closed.

The air was expelled from my lungs when I landed on my bare butt just inside the coral reef. I coughed and gasped for air, and watched the wave, its momentum broken by the reef, as it washed against the remains of the Isabeya boardwalk, sending a spray of water shooting high in the air.

Then the sea was once again calm.

Half-swimming, half-crawling, I made my way through the shallows to the beach on the backside of Harborview.

I felt for the lanyard around my neck. Moving the key chain to my salt-chapped lips, I tried to blow the London bobby's whistle.

But the feeble sound I made was lost in the muffled boom of an explosion at sea. I sat stupefied, gazing through salt-slit eyes at a brief fireball that stained the darkening sky red-orange.

Chapter
44

"HEY, KELLY, DID you see that explosion?"

I looked up to see Doug, the harbormaster, standing over me with his hands on his hips and an amused look on his face. "Kelly, what are you doing butt naked on my beach?"

I was too tired to do or say anything. I opened my mouth, but couldn't make a sound. I sat on the sand with my head cocked, staring at Doug.

"Kelly, are you drunk?"

If I tried to shake my head, I knew it would fall off my neck. The pain was back, worse than before.

"Don't move. I'll be right back." Doug sprinted in the direction of his cottage.

To preserve what little dignity I had left, I managed to get my shorts off my neck and back on my body by the time he returned with a bottle of water. He held the bottle to my lips.

I sipped the water slowly, but most of it spilled out of the corners of my mouth as it would if I'd just come home from a Novocaine session at the dentist.

"Come on, Kelly, I'll help you up."

"Doug, do you have a car to take me home? I've had a hell of a day."

We walked around the back of Harborview to the spot where his dinghy was pulled up on the beach, near what had been the water-sports pavilion before Gilda trashed it. When we reached the Dockside boardwalk, I saw Jerry talking to Victoria. He ran to the edge of the boardwalk to help me out of the dinghy.

"Kel, did you feel that quake? It rattled the dinner dishes off my table. Where have you been? You look like hell."

"Jerry, it's been a day. Can someone please take me home?"

I woke on top of my bed fourteen hours later, still in my salt-crusted clothes, to find Minx curled in a ball at my side.

I walked to the kitchen to feed Minx and open a Tab for myself. I headed outside to turn on the generator, then went to hibernate in my shower. I never thought I'd get the salt out of my hair and skin. The back of my skull was tender, but my headache was finally gone.

When I emerged from the shower, I slathered an entire bottle of lotion on my body. I looked in the full-length mirror and saw that my butt was covered with ugly bruises. I rummaged through my drawer for the softest, oldest pair of shorts I owned and a clean T-shirt. The orange shorts and ratty T-shirt went straight in the trash.

Minx sat next to her empty food bowl. "Minx, I already fed you. Do you want more?" I put a second helping of food in her dish and popped a fresh Tab for myself.

I turned off the generator and went to the gallery slab to sit and think in the quiet morning air.

No one would ever believe my story. It sounded, even to me, like I'd patched the beginning of Shakespeare's *The Tempest* with the end of Melville's *Moby Dick*. I imagined Margo's incredulous reaction. "Are you telling me you were hit over the head, dragged onto a boat, taken out to sea, dumped overboard, and it was all because of a phony treasure scam concocted by Leila Mae? Who, by the way, also killed the spitter? Yeah, right, Kel, tell me another one. I think you've been out in the sun too long. It's fried your brain."

I knew at that moment exactly how Niels Larsen felt when he made the entries in his journal, and I also knew in my heart that he was telling the truth. But I still had to unravel the tangle of clues he'd left behind.

I went back in the house to find my surf mocs. There, under the liner, was the coin I'd hidden the day before.

I opened my floor safe to retrieve the coin the spitter had left behind—the one that matched the impression in Larsen's journal.

I sat on the floor with a coin in each hand, comparing them. Daddy was a damned good forger, I'll give him that much credit. If I hadn't seen the other coin, I would easily have been fooled. Had it been anyone but Leila Mae, I might have eagerly invested in the treasure hunt. Who can resist the idea of a big payoff? Especially one in jewels and gold. Such are the things that dreams are made of.

But something was nagging at me. Something I'd read recently. Was it in the book Miss Maude brought back from Denmark or in Larsen's journal? I skimmed them both, but found nothing that rang a bell. Then I remembered the afternoon I'd spent in the Caribbean collection at the library. I dug through my purse for my datebook and soon had the answer.

Daddy's fake was a work of forger's art, but he and Leila Mae hadn't done their homework. I reread the notes I'd scrawled:

"In 1849 a new monetary system was introduced into the Danish West Indies, replacing the former value of one daler = 96 skilling. The Danish daler was equated with the U.S. dollar, and divided into 100 cents."

Daddy had screwed up big-time. On the back of his coin was: "20 Daler/1920 skilling—Dansk Vestindien." Larsen's coin showed: "20 Daler/2000 cents," followed by "Dansk Vestindien." If Larsen's coin also turned out to be a fake, at least it was accurate. To the penny.

I shoved the coins back into my safe when I heard a voice calling from the bottom of the driveway.

"Kel, are you home? Get your tush out here."

I ran outside. "Hey, Margo, come on up."

"Kel, what happened to you last night? Did you get a better offer? Or did the quake get you? Where's that lime pie you promised me? I'm starving."

I pulled the pie out of the freezer and put it on the table with paper plates, plastic forks and a knife. "Have at it, sweetie, and save a big piece for me. You can take any leftovers home with you."

"The lobster man never showed. I came to give you your twenty bucks back. We'll try it again another time." Margo stopped talking and stuffed her face with pie. I did the same, remembering I hadn't eaten in twenty-four hours. When we finished there was one tiny piece left for Paul.

"Sweetie, I hate to eat and run, but Paul needs my car to get to the airport. His broke down. Something with the electrical system. It'll take more than duct tape to repair it, and God only knows when he'll be able to get it fixed. Lunch tomorrow at the Watering Hole?"

I waved to Margo as she tore down my dirt road in a cloud of dust.

I had two things on my never-ending to-do list that required immediate attention. First, I wanted to get Top Banana back; second, I needed to have a private talk with Benjamin.

Chapter
45

IT TOOK THE rest of the morning to get Top Banana back to its mooring near my house. I found it where I'd left it, with the paddle and my bottle of water. The only thing still missing was my sun visor, but I wasn't going to worry about a trifle.

I showered again, used another bottle of lotion on my alligator skin, found more clean clothes—but added laundry to my to-do list; I was definitely scraping the bottom of the clean-clothes barrel—and headed off to Benjamin's house.

Camille and Trevor were sitting on the gallery having lunch.

"Hi, Miss Kelly," said Trevor, as he ran to the car to greet me. "Would you like to have a cup of soup?"

Looking over Trevor's head, I saw Camille smile and wink.

"Trevor, I would love some soup. What kind is it?"

"You can have chicken and rice or chicken and stars. I like stars best."

"Stars sound good to me. But only if you have enough. I like rice, too."

Trevor bounded off to the kitchen to get my soup. I joined Camille on the gallery.

"How's Benjamin feeling?"

"You know how men are. He's much better, but at the same time he's worse. He thinks he should be out of bed and back to work. But when he tries to get up, he doesn't have the strength to dress himself."

"I remember when I had dengue. I didn't have the strength to lift a glass. All I did was sleep and crab about how much I hurt. I was a real pain to live with, and I live alone."

Camille laughed. "Kelly, I wanted to thank you for taking care of Trevor last Sunday. I was so concerned about Ben, I didn't have time to think about Trevor." She looked around to make sure we weren't being overheard, then lowered her voice. "Trevor told me about the talk you two had on the beach."

"I hope I wasn't interfering."

She put her hand on my arm. "Not at all. I'm grateful you were there. Trevor told me about your talk and how you didn't make him feel like a baby when he cried. That means a lot to me. Trevor needs to know it's okay to show his feelings."

"Everything's okay with Trevor?"

"He's fine. He's been making soup for Ben and reading him stories for the past week. I may have to take him over to Amelia's tomorrow so Ben can get some rest."

Benjamin's voice called from inside the house. "Camille, who are you talking to?"

"Kelly's here, Ben. She came by to see how you were feeling."

"Bring her in here, Camille. I want to talk to her."

Camille led the way to their bedroom. "Excuse the mess, Kelly."

"Who's got time to clean after a hurricane?" We both smiled.

Benjamin was sitting up in bed with a pile of pillows behind his back. I remembered that about dengue. Not being able to get comfortable. Many nights I slept with a hot-water bottle against my back. An empty soup mug sat on the table at his side. He handed the mug to Camille. "Tell Trevor I've had enough soup for today. I'm getting waterlogged." He turned to me. "What's going on, Kelly?"

I pulled a chair next to Benjamin's bed and began to talk. I talked nonstop for half an hour while Benjamin listened intently and nodded from time to time. I told him everything. About the spitter, about the coin, about Larsen's journal, about my trip in Top Banana. And finally about Leila Mae and Daddy.

When I finally finished, Trevor poked his head in the door. He had a soup mug in his hand. "Your soup's getting cold."

"Trevor, Kelly will eat her soup later. We need to talk now. Why don't you bring us each a glass of iced tea. And see if your mother wants one, too. Then you can go next door and play until dinner."

I drank the soup to the last drop. "He's a good kid, Benjamin. I really like him."

"He likes you, too, Kelly. Thanks for having that little talk with him."

Trevor came back with two large glasses of tea. "I didn't know if you wanted sugar, so I left it plain."

"Thanks. I've got some sweetener in my purse. Your soup was delicious." I handed him the empty mug.

Trevor hugged his dad, then went out to play. Camille came to the door. "Ben, I'm going next door with Trevor. I'll be back in an hour. Thanks for coming by, Kelly. Come back anytime. We're always glad to see you."

Benjamin put down his glass when he heard the front

door slam. "You're right, Kelly. That is an incredible
story. If it were told to me by anyone else, I'd think they
were on drugs. But I know you. And I believe you. Doug
came by earlier this morning to tell me about some wreckage that had washed up on the beach during the night.
There's no doubt that the boat you described was the one
that blew up after the quake yesterday afternoon. I'm going to tell him there's no need to investigate any further.
That's one we can write off as bad seamanship."

I felt as if a weight the size of Everest had been lifted
from my shoulders.

"Thank you, Benjamin."

"Don't thank me. I should be thanking you. You're the
one she deviled the most. That woman was trouble this
time, and she was trouble when she was here before.
Some people are just born bad. The fruit never falls far
from the tree. Don't ever doubt that evil exists, Kelly. And
don't believe for one minute that bunk the preachers spout
about love and understanding changing evil to good. It
just isn't so. I'm very glad to see the last of her. Maybe
Gilda blew us some good after all." He handed me his
empty glass. "Could I trouble you for more tea?"

I filled our glasses and helped Benjamin rearrange his
pillows. "Have you tried a hot-water bottle? It worked for
me."

Benjamin's dubious glance told me he'd rather bite his
silver bullet than submit to such coddling.

"About that other matter, Kelly, I don't suppose . . ."
His eyes twinkled in anticipation.

I reached into my tote bag and handed him Larsen's
journal and the coins. "I thought you'd never ask."

Benjamin opened the book reverently. "To think this
was written by a man here in St. Chris almost 150 years
ago."

I nodded. "I know. I feel the same way about it."

I sipped my tea while he slowly turned the pages.

"Have you shared this with Miss Maude?"

"Not yet."

"Why not?"

"It's complicated, Benjamin. She was the first one I wanted to tell. But at the same time I didn't want to share it with anyone."

"Like the man who keeps a priceless painting hidden in a closet where only he can see it."

"Something like that. I guess I wanted it to be real. I believe in Niels Larsen, and I didn't want anyone to burst my bubble by telling me the journal was a fake or that Larsen never existed."

"Do you think the treasure is real?"

I nodded. "I do."

"Do you know where it is?"

"I think so. At least I know where it should be, where it was put originally. Whether it's still there?" I shrugged. "And there's the legal matter of ownership. If it's where I think it is, it's on private property. I really want the owner to have it. I'm not looking for it for myself."

"Have you said anything to this person?"

"No. I didn't want to get anyone's hopes up or cause problems for the owner. Maybe we should just leave it alone and forget about it."

Benjamin thought for a minute. "I do not agree. If it exists, we must find it before word gets out. You remember what Benjamin Franklin said? 'Three can keep a secret if two of them are dead.' I think it is obvious that two people who knew of the possibility of this treasure are now dead because of their own wickedness, and another was killed because of her own small part in it. You were very lucky to have escaped death yesterday yourself. But who knows if that luck will continue? My job is to prevent crime, not encourage it by turning a blind eye."

I had to agree with him. What Benjamin said made sense.

Benjamin looked more like his old self than he had in a week. "So, Kelly. When do you propose we look, and how can I help?"

Chapter
46

AT BENJAMIN'S INSISTENCE, Camille took Trevor over to Amelia's house to spend the night, and I was sent to summon Miss Maude.

Miss Maude and I sat with Benjamin in his living room, chatting over a picnic supper Miss Maude provided. When we finished eating, I once again told the story of Larsen's journal, omitting any mention of Leila Mae and Daddy or Leila Mae's involvement in the spitter's death. Those details Benjamin decreed were irrelevant and best forgotten. Along with finding the fake coin.

Miss Maude examined the journal carefully. "On superficial examination, I would agree this is authentic. The ink and paper appear to be of the right period. Even the handwriting and sentence construction are those of a man educated in Denmark in the mid-nineteenth century. How very much my dear papa would have enjoyed seeing this volume."

"Can you tell us if Niels Larsen really existed?" I asked.

"I may have something at home that would be of use.

Many years ago, I think it was after the 1928 hurricane, the women from the churches on St. Chris organized a project to record all the tombstones in the cemeteries located throughout the island. Quite often letters would arrive from abroad requesting information about distant family members who may have emigrated here. It was a laborious undertaking, but in the end we were successful in completing our mission. I'll look for it tonight when I return home." She reached over to pat my hand. "My dear, I applaud your resourcefulness. You have uncovered quite a treasure."

Benjamin laughed. "No treasure yet. For that we must wait another day."

"Do you think the treasure really exists?" asked Miss Maude.

"I'm sure of it," I replied. "Or at least it did in 1867."

"I also feel certain it does," added Miss Maude. "I have lived on this island for many, many years—since I was a young girl. I've lived through the Danish times and the decades after the transfer. If such a treasure had been found during my time here, I would have heard of it. We all know how people on St. Chris love to talk."

"Of tonight there will be no talk," said Benjamin sternly.

After Miss Maude left for home, I had a final word with Benjamin.

"Don't worry, Kelly. I'll take care of all the necessary arrangements tomorrow morning. Stop here when you're through at the station, and we'll synchronize our watches."

"I'll be here right after lunch. Look for me about two."

I fell asleep that night counting gold coins instead of sheep.

Chapter
47

WE ASSEMBLED AT Dockside at eight o'clock Monday night, two hours after curfew. The National Guard had blocked the roads in and out of Isabeya and more guard officers formed a cordon around the front of the hotel, extending from Kongens Gade to the ocean end of the boardwalk.

Miss Maude stood by in her capacity as the honorary Danish counsel, Benjamin represented the police, Victoria was there as Dockside's owner and me—I was hoping I hadn't made a flaming ass of myself. Victoria squeezed my hand in moral support. Her palm was clammy.

Dockside's generators were running full blast and every light on the front of the hotel was blazing. Auxiliary lights were aimed at the hotel entrance. A construction crew had worked all day to clear the storm debris from the Lower Deck courtyard.

Miss Maude had already confirmed that Niels Larsen, born March 23, 1835, Copenhagen, Denmark/died November 29, 1867, St. Cristofero, Danish West Indies, was indeed buried in the Isabeya Lutheran cemetery.

I walked toward the yellow ballast and brick staircase with a crowbar in one hand and a flashlight in the other.

I put down the crowbar and examined the stairs leading to the second-floor entrance. They were as solid as the Great Pyramid of Giza, with the bricks so tightly fitted that not even a scrap of paper could slip between them.

I walked around to the Kongens Gade side of the hotel with my small, but very attentive, audience of three following close behind me.

"In 1867, when Niels Larsen was the customs inspector, his office was the building that now houses the St. Chris library. He mentions in his journal that he was walking up the steps to his office when the earthquakes began. At first I thought he would have chosen his own building as a hiding place. We know he was waiting for the shipment of new currency to arrive from Denmark and that the bank had been severely damaged by the hurricane in late October and again by the earthquake three weeks later."

Miss Maude gave me an encouraging smile.

"I've studied photographs and sketches from the past. The library looks the same today on the outside as it did when it was the Customs House. I asked myself, if I were Niels Larsen, where would I hide something big, something very heavy? I'd put it close to the ground, and I'd put it in a place where I could keep watch on it. It had to be someplace he could easily see from his office window. And someplace not far from the ship itself, which had washed up at the foot of Kongens Gade. The men were working at night, there was no moon and no lights in town because the gas works had been shut down after the hurricane. Many of the men were sick and dying of fever. The job had to be done quickly and with a minimum of effort."

Benjamin began coughing into his handkerchief. My

years in show biz told me to get on with it and pick up the pace; I was losing my audience.

"Larsen gave us two vital clues. He wrote 'As long as mortal man may tread upon our shores, his eyes shall never see it. I raise my goblet to the success of our labors. Vive la France.' "

Benjamin stuffed his handkerchief in his pocket. "I've been reading those lines to myself all day long. What do they mean?"

I couldn't keep from smiling. "When Larsen wrote 'tread,' I assumed he was referring to walking. But tread is also defined as the upper surface of a step in a stair. If that was the case, the phrase 'tread upon our shores' could only refer to a staircase close to the sea. There are two seaside staircases in this part of Isabeya. The welcoming arms staircase at the library, which we all know is completely open on both sides and supported by the arches so beloved by the Danes, but offers no enclosed hiding places whatsoever other than a temporary shelter from the rain. And this one."

I tapped my flashlight on the side wall of the Dockside staircase. "I think this is where Niels Larsen hid the loot."

Benjamin nodded. "Very interesting. And what do we do now? Tear down the staircase?"

"No," I replied, "we look for the secret entrance."

I walked around to the far side of the staircase, the side facing the sea. The place where I'd last seen the spitter that rainy morning after the storm.

I aimed my light on the solid brick facing. I studied the arrangement of bricks and noticed a section closest to the hotel building itself that didn't quite match the overall pattern. I went up to the wall and pushed.

Nothing happened.

I tried again on a different section. Still nothing. I felt like a complete idiot.

Then I remembered Larsen's final clue: "Vive la

France." Could it have meant something more than a sa-
lute to the flag the Danish vessel had flown on its clan-
destine voyage across the Atlantic?

I totaled the number of letters in the last clue on my
fingers. Twelve. But the Dockside staircase had sixteen
steps, the same number as Howard Carter discovered in
the Valley of the Kings leading down to the tomb of Tutankhamen. Not that it had any relevance. Carter's discov-
ery was in 1922; I was trying to think like a Dane in 1867.

I went around to the front of the staircase and counted
up four stairs, down two, and up six, feeling like a kid
playing a schoolyard game. I leaned over the brick bal-
ustrade to study the wall immediately below me and noticed, for the first time, at a height comfortable for a man
of mid-nineteenth Danish stature—I've seen the colonial
military uniforms on display in the fort museum, and
those men were not giants—a finger hole in one of the
bricks. It looked as much a part of the wall as the brick
itself.

I aimed my flashlight on the brick. "Vic, point your
light where I've got mine and hold it there. I'm coming
right down."

I ran to the side of the staircase, reached up, put my
index finger in the hole and pulled.

A section of the wall, smaller than a hatch cover but
big enough for the slender hips of a Danish soldier or an
undernourished woman, swung outward.

I stuck my head inside to shine my flashlight around
the interior.

"Can you see anything?" asked Benjamin.

"What is in there, Kelly?" Miss Maude's voice was
quavering with excitement.

Victoria said nothing.

I remembered what Howard Carter had said to Lord
Carnarvon and Lady Evelyn Herbert when he first looked
into the tomb of Tutankhamen.

I turned to my friends and said, "Yes. I see wonderful
things."

Chapter
48

THE TRUTH WAS, I saw nothing of the sort. When I looked inside what I really saw was a circular brick structure about three feet high and four feet across that looked like an old well capped with more brick.

On the brick floor next to the well was a tattered paper cup and a crumpled chip bag. A far cry from the "strange animals, statues, and gold—everywhere the glint of gold" that Carter described in his journal. If I expected to find evidence of prior explorers, such as "Belzoni 1818" written in lampblack on the burial chamber wall in the pyramid of Chephren or "Blackbeard was here 1716," I was rudely disappointed.

"I lied. There's nothing in there but an old well. I think we've struck out," I said. Victoria looked like she was about to cry.

"Let me look," said Benjamin, edging me aside to stick his head in the opening. He finally turned to me and said, "it's a dead end. Nice try, Kelly."

Miss Maude spoke up. "May I have a look?" Benjamin

moved aside and gave her his torch. When she finally withdrew, her cheeks were flushed. "Kelly, you are quite mistaken. That is not a well. No one would ever have been foolish enough to sink a well this close to the sea. The water would be brackish and unfit for consumption. That is your treasure chest."

Victoria produced a step stool, and I popped through the opening with my light and crowbar.

It took the rest of the night to clear the chamber of its contents.

First, Victoria and I—we were the only ones small enough to fit inside—had to pry away the top layer of bricks. We passed them out, one by one, to Benjamin and Miss Maude. When the cover stones were removed, we finally saw the ends of the wine kegs that had held the treasure since it was first packed in Denmark for transport to the West Indies.

I knew then what Niels Larsen meant when he said "I raise my goblet to the success of our labors." I hoped that night he had toasted his achievement with more than words.

There were twelve kegs in all. When we pried open the lid of the first, we all gasped at the sight of gold. There were more coins in the kegs than one person could count in a single sitting.

By the time the last keg had been transported in an armored truck to the bank for storage in the vault, and the bricks had been neatly stacked under the stairs and the outer opening shut and sealed, it was almost five o'clock in the morning.

Victoria, Benjamin, Miss Maude and I walked upstairs to the Posh Nosh bar to fetch the bottles of champagne Victoria had put on ice at midnight.

Carrying our glasses and the unopened champagne, we strolled across the green to the old Customs House just as the roosters were beginning to crow.

We sat at the top of the welcoming arms staircase, looking first at Dockside and then at the placid ocean before us.

Benjamin opened the first bottle and solemnly filled each glass.

We raised our glasses and Victoria made the toast, echoing the words of Niels Larsen. "Vive la France."

Chapter
49

IT'S A FUNNY thing about a sudden windfall, like winning the power ball lottery, making a killing in the stock market or inheriting a bundle. You're absolutely certain it will change your life. Maybe money can buy happiness, but it can't buy power. We've been told the lights may be back on islandwide by Christmas. Or maybe not.

At Victoria's insistence we split forty/forty the long-standing reward for the recovery of the lost shipment. She wanted me to have more, though I expected little or nothing. In the end we compromised. We gave Benjamin and Miss Maude each ten percent and Trevor a coin for his collection.

Victoria paid off her mortgage and now owns Dockside free and clear.

I paid off my own mortgage and now, like Margo said when she sweet-talked me into buying the former Danish schoolhouse, I'll never have to worry about being a bag lady.

Mrs. H, the WBZE owner, finally came back to St.

Chris from her six-month 'round-the-world cruise, speaking Italian like a native. All because of a man named Marcello who looks like Rossano Brazzi in the film version of *South Pacific* and owns a winery and villa in Tuscany. When she told me she was putting the station up for sale, I made her an offer she couldn't refuse. She took my check, kissed me on both cheeks, whispered, *"Ciao, bella"* and was off on the next plane to Rome on a one-way ticket. We promised to keep in touch and exchange fruitcakes every Christmas.

Victoria and I set up a foundation to fund a homeless shelter and rehab center. We named it after Niels Larsen.